IN STARLIGHT

FEBRUARY GRACE

Booktrope Editions
Seattle, WA 2014

COPYRIGHT 2014 FEBRUARY GRACE

This work is licensed under a Creative Commons Attribution-Noncommercial-No Derivative Works 3.0 Unported License.
Attribution — You must attribute the work in the manner specified by the author or licensor (but not in any way that suggests that they endorse you or your use of the work).
Noncommercial — You may not use this work for commercial purposes.
No Derivative Works — You may not alter, transform, or build upon this work.

Inquiries about additional permissions
should be directed to: info@booktrope.com

Cover Design by Ida Jansson

This is a work of fiction. Names, characters, places, brands, media, and incidents are either the product of the author's imagination or are used fictitiously. Any resemblance to similarly named places or to persons living or deceased is unintentional.

PRINT ISBN 978-1-62015-346-8

EPUB ISBN 978-1-62015-371-0

Library of Congress Control Number: 2014907417

*This book is dedicated with affection to every reader
who asked for 'more about Gus and Till'.*

Thank you.

Chapter One

Secrets

Daybreak, January 1, 2013

ANGUS CAILAN DUNCAN WAS ABOUT TO DO the hardest thing he had ever done in his life. He was going to walk out on the woman he loved, after one perfect night in her arms.

Worse, he was going to do so immediately after making a sincere and heartfelt marriage proposal he knew he could not follow through on, no matter how much he wanted to.

"How I wish ye'd be able to remember just this one thing: that I am goin' to love ye with all I am, the rest of my days," he whispered. As he closed the heavy, antique door between them, his heart shattered with the sound — crushed by the weight of not only his own sorrow, but the depth of hers.

No matter how old he lived to be, no matter what else he recalled about the night his One Wish was fulfilled, the memory of Till's anguished sobs would override every happier thought.

He hurried up the stairs and into his apartment, so distraught he didn't even consider using his magical talents to transport himself there.

He paused for a moment before the bay window. His eyes blurred as he stared out at the falling snow. Everything was painted white with it; the grasping tree branches, barren flower beds, rolling land outside, all hibernating beneath a shimmering, crystal blanket.

Never in his life could he remember a winter that felt so long.

As anxious as he was to see the sun return, he didn't know how he could ever appreciate its warmth the same way again; now that he knew for certain the coldest night in winter could burn brighter than the hottest summer day.

The tremor began at his knees and spread furiously through his body. He shuddered a slow, painful breath. He shook in deep, gutting waves that caused his teeth to clamp together behind lips still stinging from the absence of her kiss.

He stripped away his clothes, starting with the shirt he had never bothered to button. His black kilt, boots, everything was tossed aside as he went into the bath and turned on a blazing hot shower.

He leaned against the wall for support, at times fearing that he lacked the ability to keep to his feet. No matter how long he stood in the water and rising steam, he couldn't get warm.

He ached. He didn't know how he would ever face Till again, with the knowledge that she loved him too but could not say.

Not only did he have to figure out how he was going to face her, but he had to come up with a way to keep his emotions from her day by day as they worked together. *Every day. For the rest of their lives.*

Maybe Lane had been right, he thought, though he hated to admit the possibility. *Maybe we should have heeded his objections to our pairing as partners. Maybe the past blinded me to the truth that he knew better this time.* Everything in Gus railed against the thought. No, he couldn't accept that.

He knew that he could never give Till up. To ask that would be asking him to abandon what little remained of his damaged soul.

After what seemed an eternity, his shaking finally slowed. The ancient tank in the basement ran out of hot water, and he shivered anew as he turned the tap and toweled off.

He dressed for the day and once again stood before the window, trying to figure out what he was supposed to do now.

He knew he couldn't call in sick to the bookstore. As hard as it would be to face Till today, he believed the longer it took between this moment and the time when he looked in her eyes again, and saw that she viewed him as she always had — with no memory of their perfect, shared night — the harder it would be on him. He also knew calling in would put Mrs. Nesbitt, Till's mother and manager of the store, in a terrible spot. So he would do the only thing he could. He'd soldier on.

* * *

Mrs. Nesbitt scanned him suspiciously as he stood there, staring blankly at the time clock. "You okay, Gus? You look awfully pale this morning."

"I'm not feelin' a hundred percent, Missus."

She frowned. "I hope you're not coming down with whatever Till has. She called in sick."

"Did she now?" Gus was puzzled by this. It had been hours since he'd left Till; she should've been ready to face the day as usual, with only perhaps the trace of a headache from crying too long and confusion over why she'd been crying at all. "I hope she feels better soon, whatever she's sufferin' through."

"Me too, and I hope you escape whatever is ailing you."

Not bloody likely, Gus thought, as he attempted to mask his pain with a failed smile. "Many thanks."

He went through the motions of the work day without really hearing or seeing anyone or anything that crossed his path. Everyone appeared lifeless; as one-dimensional as the store's cardboard displays.

He kept checking his watch, and promised himself that the moment he punched out again he would take an evening for himself; to remember, to grieve, and try, somehow, to pull himself together to face tomorrow.

When quitting time finally came, he drove back to the house and parked his truck. The biting chill in the air gnawed at his bones, and he leaned across the seat to reach for the gloves and scarf scattered there. When he picked up the scarf, he felt his breath catch. Till had borrowed it just two days before, and the aroma of rose water clung to it: her soft, subtle perfume.

His heart raced on without mercy. He lowered the scarf around his neck and drew its end close to his face, inhaling her scent.

God, Tilda Mae, I miss ye so much.

He knew now what he needed to do.

He needed to take a long walk on a lonely beach.

* * *

His destination was well in mind before he set foot upon the soil; Barleycove Beach, in County Cork.

He hoped the sight of familiar hills in the distance would warm his heart just a little; but the fog was so thick he could barely make them out.

He considered a trip to nearby Mizen Head to see the signal light, but knew even that faithful beacon could not help him find his way this time. He'd already crashed into the rocks full force, and nothing could save him from this heartache of his own creation.

His grief not only blocked out the rest of the world but held him captive inside himself; a prisoner of emotions he never wanted to have.

He never meant to fall in love with Till.

In the beginning he'd just wanted to watch out for her, for Aunt Tilda's sake. To teach her as best he could, and hope she wouldn't lose herself entirely to her new role as a Fairy Godmother. What he didn't expect was for her to grow into the role so perfectly it was as though it was tailored to her very soul.

As though she was tailored to *his* very soul.

She was so generous. She always tried her best on every assignment, with every duty required. She was grateful for every blessing bestowed, no matter how small.

Till could make nothing feel like everything, and had made his feelings of affection ignite from spark to conflagration in what seemed a matter of moments.

He'd been in love with her a lot longer than he was willing to admit to himself, until now. Even when he'd been holding her, kissing her and finally, last night fulfilling his One Wish and making love to her, he wasn't ready to accept just how dear and desperately needed a part of him she had become.

Till didn't just have his heart; she *was* his heart.

Now he had to learn to live with the knowledge that everywhere he went, everything he did, and every secret he kept, his heart would dwell forever just beyond his reach.

He was a ghost now; haunting this life and haunted by love in the form of a tall, sweet girl with light brown hair, little black glasses perched upon her nose, and the same pink high-top shoes always upon her feet, even when she'd dressed up for graduation.

She'd looked so beautiful in that pure white dress; her fair shoulders visible to him for the first time. How he'd longed to kiss them, and the lovely neck adorned with the gift he'd given her at Christmas. A gift that held every bit of the significance that he'd been so afraid to assign to it. It *was* meant to symbolize the key to his heart.

Gus stopped walking and looked down at his boot prints in the sand. He glanced back at the long line he'd left behind as he'd walked, and thought that though all anyone else would ever see were one lonely pair of wandering feet, to his eyes another set appeared to trail alongside.

Wherever he was, Till would be. After last night, there was no way she could ever be out of his mind or heart, no matter what the future held for them.

All at once Gus felt as if he was at serious risk of dissolving down to nothing in the Atlantic's advancing tide.

Time to move on, he thought. *Somewhere else I need to go.*

* * *

Soon he was standing in a familiar cemetery in Scotland, gaze cast down upon his parents' grave.

He dropped to his knees and, as was his custom in the winter, he cleared the dusting of snow away before he did or said anything. His eyes moved over the names inscribed in stone: *Katherine Mary O'Sullivan-Duncan,* and *Alec Angus Duncan.*

"Ah, Katie," he whispered, wishing he could feel his mother's energy around him now. If she had been granted the peaceful fairies' demise that he felt she was due, he should have been able to sense her presence, still; but the penalties for disobedience were severe, and unkind. "Why didn't ye give me the surname O'Sullivan, after yer family? Why curse me with the Duncan name, and the destiny that seems to accompany it?" He pointed to his father's name next. "The Duncan family motto..." He sighed heavily. "*Learn To Suffer*? So I am. I wonder if this is how the pair of ye suffered, before ye finally gave into it."

He dropped his head into his hands. After a while, he shook freshly fallen snow from his hair and stood once more. "Yeah. I much prefer the O'Sullivan motto." He conjured a single rose and left it in the vase at the base of the headstone. *"The Steady Hand To Victory."*

He took a few steps forward, but then turned back.

"I think I understand why ye did it now. Why ye broke the rules and gave into lovin' each other… and I…" He said something now he didn't ever imagine he'd say. "I forgive ye for it."

Chapter Two
Hide and Seek

April 2, 2013

"CATCH ME IF YE CAN, LITTLE GIRL…" Gus taunted under his breath. He watched as Till wandered aimlessly about twenty feet from his current position.

Their strength as a team continued to grow steadily day by day, but Gus saw no reason why they shouldn't have a bit of fun tonight, and hone her skills while they were at it. They had no other pressing business to attend to, so he'd suggested a round of the Fairy Godparent equivalent of an old children's game: he'd hide and she'd seek.

Only to complicate things, he wasn't just hiding in the house, or even in the same state. The options for where to go this time were open world-wide, and he planned to make it a very interesting exercise.

Till was beginning to get frustrated, and he found it absolutely adorable though he'd never admit it to her. Even if he were allowed to share such feelings with her, he knew her well enough by now to understand that the idea of being cute when annoyed would only make her more upset.

"Where are you…?" she mumbled. He read her lips through the glass and fought the urge to laugh. She was so close now, but he'd shielded himself from her thoughts just enough that she couldn't easily see him mixed in among the mannequins in the display. Or so he thought.

A second later she was standing next to him, tapping a pink-shoed foot. "Window at Harrods? Really? This is the beginner level of the game?"

Gus did laugh now; a low, soft rumble.

"Mum, look!" a child cried, knocking on the glass and pointing wildly at Till and Gus as his mother focused on her phone. "The mannequins are alive! They're moving!"

"That's lovely, darling," the mother said, totally oblivious.

Gus gave the boy a small wave and winked at Till. "Level two…" he said, and then he was gone; leaving the child with his mouth hanging open and a mind full of questions.

Gus next popped up inside the Louvre; followed by a quick stop at the Arc de Triomphe after deciding the Eiffel Tower would be entirely too obvious a choice.

"Ah, Paris in springtime," Till grinned as she touched him on the shoulder. "How about it's my turn now?"

Gus raised an eyebrow. "Go on, then, Tilda Mae. Show me what ye've got."

Till giggled as she vanished, and Gus took a moment to catch his breath and refocus his energy on shielding parts of his mind from her that would be dangerous for her to go near. "I shouldn't have brought her here," he whispered to himself, leaning back against the nearest wall. "She outshines the City of Light."

As beautiful as his surroundings were, their impact was lost on him. Winter had felt eternal, now spring was hollow — a grayed-out shadow of expected splendor. How else could it seem without her love?

He closed his eyes a moment and tuned in as best he could on the signature trail that Till had left. She was good, but not so good yet that he couldn't find her with relative speed.

He strode up to her, grinning, as she stood on an Old Town Edinburgh street, trying to catch her breath.

"Drat it, you found me."

"Maybe ye should've taken the low road."

Till scoffed. "Brat. Okay, here we go. I hope you're in the mood for a walk." She made sure the coast was clear and then, she vanished.

He next found her behind a stand of poplar trees on a rolling Irish hill. For a moment the sight caught Gus off guard. He had not been back to Ireland since New Year's Day.

"All right, ye have proved y'er learnin'," he said, also starting to tire. "Enough for tonight."

"Awww, c'mon," Till nudged him gently with her elbow. "Just a couple more?"

He sighed. He couldn't say no to her, at least not when it wasn't absolutely necessary. "Very well. One more, then the last one is mine."

Till squealed and then disappeared.

Gus followed the breadcrumb trail through her thoughts, and the next time he looked up, he was amazed by what he saw.

He was standing in a theme park before a life-sized castle, with fireworks soaring overhead. Families with small children were everywhere. He turned around and gazed upon Till, her face alight in the glow of the nighttime spectacular with the same wonder he saw in the faces of the children.

He approached her and shook his head. Only she would bring them here.

"A magical place, indeed," Gus said, the edge of his lip curling slightly as he considered how little the Hollywood version of Fairy Godparents matched the reality. Till surprised him by reaching over and looping her arm around his.

"It is so beautiful."

She was standing closer to him than he was comfortable with now, and memories he had to hide from her flooded his mind. He was overwhelmed by the thought of her hands moving over his shoulders...her arms wrapped around him. Her passionate kiss, her gentle caress. Everything that made his One Wish so perfect, and would keep it as fresh in his memory in a hundred years as it was the night it had all taken place.

"We... better go," Gus said, gently withdrawing his arm. "Last one's mine." Then he was gone.

Till obediently followed, though when she located him again she didn't look happy, she looked unsettled.

He'd decided to hide last of all in a secluded place behind the Music building at Dreams Come True University; a lovely little spot skirted by trees and flowers.

"What's the matter then?" he asked, concerned as all the color drained from her face.

"Game over..." Till's voice faded along with the blush in her cheek, and her thoughts grew faint as well.

He was alarmed; he could not recall her mind ever becoming so unreadable, so quickly, in the

past. Sure, a deeper thought might be replaced by one a bit more trivial and he'd know that she wished to change the subject, but never all of her thoughts completely dying away as they just had. He stopped short of placing a hand on her shoulder. "Are ye all right, Till?"

"Yeah." She ran her hands up and down her arms as if to warm them, though it was as comfortable a temperature as ever on campus. "Can we just call it a night?"

"Sure thing." Gus wondered at the change in her mood. He had no idea why being in this particular place should cause her to shut down so completely. "Let's go on home."

An instant later they were standing in the driveway of the house on Finch Street.

"Good night," she said, hurrying up the steps and through the doorway before he had a chance to say — or ask — anything more.

Chapter Three
Another Story to Tell

GUS GLANCED UP AT THE CLOCK on the wall for the tenth time in the past hour. His shift was almost over at the bookstore, but that wasn't what had him distracted. He sensed Till's presence drawing near, and she wasn't alone.

Another woman fell into step beside her as Till strode from the sales floor into the back room. That woman was, for lack of a better word, whining.

It was a familiar whine, but Gus would have known that it was his housemate and Till's tenant, Hannah, even if he hadn't heard her signature squeaking. Her very presence in a room was enough to declare her neediness.

"Just one day," Hannah pleaded. "I can't get another advance from Lane, and my tips don't get paid out of the pool until tomorrow..."

Till's glare accompanied thoughts that Gus could clearly read. She was wondering where Hannah's rent money had gone this month. Shoes? A handbag she just had to have? Of every fairy Gus had ever met, Hannah's tastes were the most frivolous, and her self-control the most non-existent.

"Tomorrow, Hannah. By five. I'm serious this time." Till could never really bring herself to say no to Hannah's pleas for an extension on the due date for her rent— and worried what would happen to her if she ended up with a much more business-minded landlady.

"You're a lifesaver. Thanks, Till." Hannah tried to hug Till, but Till recoiled like a cat dragged toward a bathtub.

"You're welcome."

Hannah waved to Gus, who gave her a casual salute as she rushed past him and toward the back door.

She suddenly whirled around to face Till again. "By the way, have either of you noticed that Lane is acting even stranger than usual lately?"

"How do ye mean?" Gus asked, alarmed. Till leaned against the wall beside his desk and just listened.

"He's been asking all kinds of weird questions. Poking his nose into things that don't concern him. Once or twice, I could have sworn he'd been following me around after work." Hannah shuddered. "It's really starting to creep me out."

"If ye'd like, I'll have a word with him," Gus offered.

Till raised her hand to object. "That's very chivalrous of you, Gus, but if anyone should talk to Lane about this, it's me. It's my job." She nodded toward Hannah. "If he gives you any more trouble, let me know." Her voice wavered slightly, and Gus could feel that she was putting on a brave front for some reason. The idea of talking to Lane had her rattled.

"Thanks, Till, you're the best!" Hannah blew kisses to both of them and then she was gone.

Gus sighed. "I really wish ye'd let me talk to him, Till." Lane could be more trouble than he thought Till realized, and felt he should be the one to step in.

"If I change my mind, I'll let you know, okay?"

He looked at her doubtfully.

"I promise."

"Very well." Gus slowly returned his eyes to the computer screen so he'd be forced to stop staring at her. He tried to lighten the moment. "Kind of ye, givin' Hannah another extension on her rent. What would happen to that girl if she didn't have ye lookin' out for her the way that ye do?"

"I think that Aunt Tilda worried about that, too. That's why she, and I, both put up with Hannah's shenanigans."

"Try sayin' that three times fast." He glanced up from the screen and over at her again. She had just put on a new raincoat that accompanied a hat so lovely, Gus thought he might melt at the sight. He came back to the moment as her tone changed.

"Have *you* noticed anything strange about Lane lately?"

Lane is always strange, Gus thought. He quickly swept the observation away before she caught it. He sat up straighter in his chair, shoulders thrust back. Just as he feared, there was more to that quiver in her voice than she had wanted to let on to Hannah. "Why? Has he been hasslin' ye too?"

"I wouldn't so much call it 'hassling' as I would just... making me uncomfortable," Till said. The look on Gus's face must have spooked her, because suddenly she seemed to think better of continuing the conversation. "You know what? Forget I said anything. I have to go."

Anger rose in Gus and it crept into his voice. "Till, if he's harassin' you in *any* way—"

"Really, it's all right. I can handle it."

He hurried to log off of his computer and rose from his chair. "I think we should talk about this some more. Over a bite at Maizey's?" He knew the little diner down the block was always irresistible to Till. She rocked back and forth slowly, considering.

"Well... I noticed their menu board as I walked past earlier, and they do have chicken pie tonight." She hesitated. "Do we have time before we get to work for the evening? I don't have anything on my schedule, but you must have something on yours that we need to see to."

"We'll make the time," Gus declared, reinforcing the words with a thought directed straight at her that indicated he was not going to take no for an answer. "I have an appointment to see Ryan on my own. Have a bit of a man-to-man with him. Seems he's in some trouble at school and they're havin' a meetin' about it. But not until later." He didn't realize he was still staring at Till until her expression questioned what it was he was looking at as she nervously straightened her hat. Gus reddened slightly, averting his eyes as he grabbed his jacket and umbrella. He always brought one, because Till never did.

"Well, if you're sure..."

Gus's stomach turned, feeling how uneasy she really was about the subject of Lane in general. There were parts of his history that she still didn't know, and he figured that it was finally time he told her the rest. "Absolutely." He punched out at the clock, held the back door open for her and popped open the umbrella. She smiled as he lifted it up over her head and gestured toward his 1958 Chevy pickup. "Yer chariot awaits."

* * *

Gus treasured very few possessions in life, but his truck was one of them.

He kept it very carefully, and not always by magic, either. He was often seen washing and waxing it in the summer, or working to keep the pristine interior spotless.

Till looked at him now with her lip caught between her teeth, worried, as he held open the passenger door for her in the pouring rain.

"My shoes are gonna drip all over the floor mats."

"So are mine. I'm more concerned with gettin' ye warm and dry."

She smiled and stepped up into the cab. Once she was safely inside, Gus ran around the front of the truck, opened his own door and jumped in. He shook the umbrella out as best he could before he set it down on the floor at her feet.

"Bucketin' out there…" He was so preoccupied now that he took to nervously stating the obvious. Fortunately, she was much too kind to point it out.

She nodded, and Gus sensed a shift in her thoughts and emotions as she turned toward the window. He paused with the key in the ignition and looked directly at her. "Till, ye know that ye can tell me anythin', right?"

"I know," she said, her voice rising to a small squeak. She cleared her throat and repeated the words, adding, "Thank you."

"I mean it. Anythin'."

"I'll remember that, Gus," she said in a restrained, even tone this time, all emotion fading from her voice. "Thank you."

Gus hated the singular sort of silence that fell between them now, because it was a clear indication something was really bothering her. She normally chattered on at him at a fairly regular pace; one he'd grown accustomed to, and one that still seemed to surprise her. She'd often say she never talked as much to anyone else about anything in her life as she talked to Gus.

Gus loved her chatter. The tone of her voice soothed him, and he found her distinct, Michigan-grown accent as quirky as it was charming.

Though she often spoke of many things in a short period of time, none of them were ever trivial. Till did not make small talk… well, with the exception of talking about the weather when her mother would put the two of them in a potentially embarrassing situation by trying to push them together. Then she could talk about low pressure systems and jet streams with the best of them.

The rest of the time, when it was just the two of them, her words were always substantive. That fact alone made her the most interesting person to listen to that Gus had ever known.

They arrived at the restaurant and took up their small, regular corner booth. Till said nothing, allowing Gus to order their favorite dinners, along with a pot of tea to help fend off the chill from the rain.

Till stirred her tea much longer than it took to dissolve the sugar, and Gus worried. He could feel her fear, and had to fight not to take hold of her hand to try to comfort her.

Hands off, Duncan, he chided himself, gripping his mug of tea so tight his fingers felt numb.

He allowed her to sit in silence, her thoughts spinning so quickly that he couldn't make sense of them, until their food arrived. He picked up her fork and handed it to her, gesturing with his own toward her food. "Please, Till, ye have to eat somethin'."

She poked at her plate, the expression on her face indicating she had no appetite. She scanned his features carefully, and finally took a tentative bite. She consumed it thoughtfully before hitting him right between the eyes with a question he wasn't prepared for.

"So when are you going to tell me the truth about you and Lane?"

Gus almost inhaled his sip of tea. He cleared his throat and sat back in the booth. "How do ye mean?"

"You wanted to come here and talk about Lane, so let's talk about Lane. I asked you once what was between the two of you, why you didn't get along. You told me to pay it no mind. Well, I do mind. I wish you'd tell me."

Gus exhaled a slow sigh. *Damn, she's better at readin' my mind than I am at readin' hers these days...*

"I brought you here to tell you just that, Tilda Mae." He set down his utensils and then dropped his hands from the table. She couldn't see it, but beneath the surface he was clenching them into fists as memories stirred in him now. "If Lane is givin' anyone trouble, *especially* at home, it's time for ye to know the truth about why we don't get along."

"I can't read you now," Till whispered, leaning closer. "Was it really so bad?"

"Yeah," Gus hesitated. He'd hated the thought that this moment was ever going to come, and here it was. He was going to have to tell her the truth about his troubled history with Lane. "It was that bad. Ye see, Lane and I, we worked together in my first year out of university."

"You're not telling me that he was your mentor!" She struggled to keep her voice down as she reached out and grasped hold of the sleeve of his jacket.

"Aye, he was, and he didn't handle the position well." He shifted and began drawing imaginary circles on the top of the table just to give him something else to look at beside the distress in her eyes. "I don't know if ye've noticed, but Lane has a thing about power."

"Yeah, that 'thing' being that when he gets a little of it, he goes nuts with it," Till replied. "What happened, Gus? What *really* happened?"

"He made my life a livin' hell, is what happened," Gus explained. He ran a hand back through his hair and then shifted again in his seat. He couldn't seem to sit still. "No matter what I did, it wasn't fast enough. Good enough. Smart enough. Got to the point where he almost got us caught once in public, dressin' me down so loud that people could hear."

"Oh my God," Till whispered. "What did you do?"

"I didn't do anythin'. I figured it was just the way that it was, being the younger partner. But Aunt Tilda, she got out of me what happened and took it upon herself to intervene."

"No way."

"Yeah. She reported him to the university. He was disciplined, suspended for a year from the program, and removed as my mentor, immediately. After that they didn't bother assignin' me a new one, said I was doin' fine on my own. So on my own, I went forward."

"Wow." Till shook her head. "I never expected that." She looked him straight in the eyes. "How is it that you've managed to keep this from me all this time? I mean, I have seen a lot of what goes on in there," she pointed in the general direction of his head. "I can't believe I didn't figure this one out."

"Ye didn't figure it out because I didn't want ye to."

Her expression changed again; now she was hurt. She clearly didn't like the idea of him keeping things from her on purpose. She seemed to be overreacting, though, in Gus's estimation. She'd always known that as they worked more closely together, more and more frequently he would have thoughts she couldn't get to, and she would have thoughts she would shield from him as well. In this instance, she just couldn't seem to understand why he felt the need to keep the information from her.

If only she knew, Gus thought sadly, *all that I am forced to keep from her.*

"I should have known this sooner, Gus," she blurted at last, pushing her plate away. "I'm responsible for what goes on in the house, and if I'd known that Lane had a history like that I would have—"

"Treated him differently. I know," Gus replied, finishing her thought. "I didn't want ye to. I figured that enough time had passed, hoped he'd learned his lesson. Thought maybe that he'd right himself and behave like a man instead of an arrogant..."

"I still wish you'd told me," Till interrupted.

"I'm sorry. I thought I was doin' the right thing." He looked at her sideways. "Now are ye goin' to be straight with me about how he's treatin' ye, or do I need to have a talk with him myself?"

"Neither," Till replied, reaching out to take the bill from the waitress as she held it between the two of them. Gus was faster, and he snatched it from her reach.

"Let me get mine, at least," Till objected.

"No, this one's on me. And why neither?" He wasn't going to let her off the hook so easily.

"Because I will handle it myself."

Now Gus was the one with wounded feelings. "We're partners, Tilda Mae. We're supposed to look out for each other. I can't do that if ye don't tell me what's wrong."

"And I can't do it without the information I need to make sound decisions," Till replied with irritation. Immediately, her eyes conveyed an unspoken apology. "I will keep you posted if he keeps it up, okay?"

Gus tossed some money and the check onto the table, watching as Till stared at her uneaten food.

"If that's what ye wish."

"It is."

"Fine."

"Fine."

"I'll drop ye off at home on the way to see Ryan."

"I can get there on my own," Till replied. "I don't want to cost you any more time tonight."

"It's on the way, Till. I... really want to see ye home."

Finally, she gave in. "All right."

* * *

Once settled into the truck, she leaned her head back against the seat and closed her eyes. She was wishing for sleep, he could feel it, and he wished that she could be afforded the luxury.

He wished *he* could be afforded the luxury.

"Know what? I think we ought to make one more stop tonight before I go on."

"Oh no, Gus, I don't..."

"I do." He merged onto the highway and drove to the Park and Ride lot. Instantly she knew what he had in mind.

Till concentrated for a moment, honing her thoughts in on her young charge, Violet. She nodded. "Looks like her parents have gone out for the evening, and the babysitter is letting her fuss in her crib." This displeased Till highly, but still she hesitated. "If you go with me, you might be late."

"Just a short visit. I can still make it."

"Thanks, Gus. I think that would be the best thing for me."

Gus wondered, sometimes, what the best thing really was for Till. He had a feeling that it was something that he was never going to be able to give her— a completely open relationship. One in which he never had to conceal a single thought or emotion from her again. He quickly tried to avert his thoughts from the path that they were taking, a path toward dangerous memories that he couldn't risk her picking up on.

How he wished a day would come when he could be everything she needed.

Chapter Four
Sweet Dreams

"WE'RE GOING TO HAVE TO DO SOMETHING about replacing that babysitter," Till grumbled, upon arrival at Violet's house. She peeked around the corner into the kitchen and observed as the teen, instead of watching over Violet like she was supposed to, clicked between browser windows on a laptop computer. One was blaring music, and the other displayed a video chat with a boy who looked questionable at best. "Anything could happen to Violet with her in charge."

"I don't like the looks of the situation, either." Gus whispered. "We'll work on it."

They made their way into Violet's room and turned off the baby monitor before gently closing the door.

The moment Violet looked up and laid eyes upon Till, she stopped fussing. She kicked tiny legs and wiggled her arms in excitement. Till reached into the crib and gently picked her up. The act had become second nature to her after their many visits here in the past few months; but the sight of Till with a baby in her arms never lost its power over Gus. It always made him more than a little sentimental; it seemed so obvious that she should be holding a baby of her own.

If only things were different, he thought. *I'd love to have one just like her. No, just like you.*

"Ever wish you could have one of your own, Gus?" Till asked suddenly, and he wondered if he'd been thinking a little too loud; just enough for her to pick up on his mood, and sense to ask the question.

He shrugged. "Doesn't everyone?"

"No, not everyone. But most people who do want to, can have one. Even if they adopt." She stopped and shrugged as well.

Gus worried. By this point it was clear to him that something besides Lane's recent behavior was weighing on her. Before he could stop himself, he thought two more words clearly to her.

Go on...

"Nothing more to say," Till replied, as she carefully set the now sleeping Violet down in her crib. "What's the point of wishing for what you can't have?"

The words stung Gus in a way that he'd never be able to explain to her, and that made it all hurt so much worse.

I do that every day, my darlin'... he thought. Quickly he forced the thought behind another, fast enough that he was certain Till missed the "my darlin'", at least.

Chapter Five
Troubled

GUS FINALLY CAUGHT UP TO RYAN in a most unhappy place: a hastily assembled, late night meeting of the local school board. He'd arrived just in time to speak on the boy's behalf, and after he finished, he hurried to usher Ryan out of the room.

"How many times can I say I'm sorry?" The young man jammed paint-stained hands into the pockets of his hooded sweatshirt. "I told them, and I'm telling you. I'm sorry!"

"Not good enough this time, Ryan. Ye should have known better, yeah?" Gus couldn't remember ever having been quite so frustrated with his teenaged charge before. Then again, he'd never had to spend so much time passionately pleading Ryan's case to the principal, vice principal, homeroom teacher, and half of the school board before. "What were ye thinkin', paintin' caricatures of the faculty on the walls of the gymnasium? Didn't ye think they'd catch ye?"

"I figured the space needed some artwork," Ryan muttered, a self-satisfied smile crossing his face just long enough to really upset Gus.

Gus stopped walking and turned to face the youth. "Do ye know what, Ryan? The world doesn't revolve around what ye figure, or what ye want. There was somewhere I wanted to be tonight. Someplace important, looking after a friend. Was I able to be there? No. I had to drop everythin' to try to keep yer sorry behind in school. And still ye came out of it with three days suspension."

Ryan smirked. "Vacation."

"NO!" Gus's temper flared, and Ryan winced. Gus had never raised his voice to the boy before, no matter what stupid stunt he'd pulled. This time, though, he'd almost ended up expelled, and it was only Gus's quick thinking and smooth talking that had gotten him out of it. He needed to understand the gravity of the situation.

"Tell me, Ryan, that there weren't going to be any gang tags on that 'artwork' when ye finished?"

Ryan looked at his shoes and kicked at the ground.

"If I find y'er gettin' into that sort of trouble, Ryan, that is where my mentorship ends," Gus warned. "Do ye think that I can save ye from yerself if y'er determined to self-destruct? Don't ye deserve better than that? Doesn't yer mother deserve better? Don't I, for lookin' after ye? What are ye thinkin', boy?"

Ryan's voice broke. "I wasn't thinking! You don't understand what it's like, Gus. Being in that school, in that neighborhood, day after day." His chest rose and fell quickly, and Gus could tell he was fighting tears. "We need to get *out*, Gus. Away from here. We need to move far away where no one knows us. Start over."

Gus's mind ran a hundred miles an hour now. If they moved far away, Ryan couldn't be his Fairy Godparenting charge any longer, because the boy was never meant to know what Gus really was. If Gus helped arrange for them to relocate, which he certainly had the ability and connections to do, he'd only get to visit the boy on the rare occasion. Another, local Fairy Godfather would have to take his place as Ryan's mentor.

At this point, though, he was unsure there was any other solution. Even though he despised the idea of turning Ryan over to someone else, keeping the boy here was clearly not the answer either. Not anymore.

"All right."

"All right, what?"

"I'll... talk to yer Ma. I know she's been wantin' to get out for a while now... I can make some phone calls, see if I can find her some work." Ryan's mother was a diner waitress, so Gus had no doubt he'd be able to secure her a job somewhere far away, and a little apartment to rent for the two of them nearby. "If I do this, are ye really gonna apply yerself to startin' over? New school, new attitude? Clean slate?"

"God, Gus, if you can help us get away from here... some place warm, and different, I swear..." Tears reddened Ryan's eyes, though they did not spill. "I swear I will become the student that you believe I can be. The one I used to be, before everything got so ugly here."

Gus nodded and placed a hand upon Ryan's shoulder. "Very well, then. I warn ye, though, things are likely to move quickly once I set them in motion, with yer Ma's okay. Ye better be prepared."

"I am so ready to get the hell out of here," Ryan declared with a nod. "I am going to miss you, though. Do you think you'll ever be able to come and visit?"

"Once in a while," Gus said, wishing it could be more often. "I'll see to it that ye get a new mentor where ye're goin'. Not going to risk ye fallin' back into old habits in new places. And I swear, boy, if I hear *one word* about ye pickin' up a can of spray paint..."

"I won't, I promise. I'll keep my art on canvas, where it belongs."

"Then I'll do my best to see that ye don't run out of canvases and sketchbooks, so."

"Really?"

"Really."

Ryan threw his arms around Gus and slapped him on the back in a manly hug. "Thanks, Gus. I, I don't know what I would have done without you all this time. I really don't."

"Then show me yer gratitude now," Gus said, releasing the boy and looking him dead in the eyes. "Show ye've earned the faith I still have in ye, and make me, and yer Ma, proud."

"I will."

"Good. Now, it's time to take ye home. I have someplace else I need to be."

* * *

Gus knocked on the door to the library. When he was invited to open it, he found Till sitting cross-legged upon the couch, staring at an empty space on the shelf across the room.

"Times like this I really wish I still had that special book," she whispered. "I'm sure there was so much more Aunt Tilda could have taught me. I..." She paused. "I miss her."

"As do I, Tilda Mae," Gus replied gently. "What would you still be needin' lessons about, then?"

"I tried talking to Lane when I got home," Till answered. She blinked quickly; an attempt to hold back tears. "It did not go well."

Gus silently cursed himself; she should never have had to face this night alone. He was angry at Lane, angry at Ryan, and most of all, angry at himself. "I'm sorry, Till. So sorry I wasn't there with ye." He moved over toward the shelf to keep himself from inching closer to her. He ran his fingertips across the surface. "Though if it's any consolation, I don't know that Aunt Tilda would've been able to anticipate and give ye any instruction as to how to deal with Lane. She always wanted to think the best of everyone, no matter what they did."

"She was a wonderful person. I wish more people were around to remember that."

Gus finally turned to face her again. "We'll remember that. She won't be forgotten." His thoughts

returned to a night last year spent beneath a star-filled sky; a night during which the Lyrids soared above, and Gus confessed to Till that he most of all feared being forgotten. She had promised him then she would never let that happen; that it couldn't happen, because there was no one else in the world like him.

If he hadn't already been in love with her before that night, he surely would have been after it.

"I wish ye'd tell me what went wrong. Maybe there is somethin' I can do to help."

"I don't think you can, but thank you," Till said, silently brushing away a stray tear that made its way down her cheek. "I will find a way to deal with it. At the very least, I hope he'll leave Hannah alone for a little while. He should be more focused on pestering me."

"I don't like that trade at all."

"Yeah, well, it is what it is."

"I wish ye'd let me help, Till. Please, I'm beggin', let me intervene."

"Not yet, all right? If anything else comes of all of this, I promise, I'll ask for your help. Right now... I just really feel like I need to stand up to him on my own."

Till looked away, and Gus knew he'd better go. If he stayed a moment longer, he risked thinking the wrong thing too far out in the open — that thing being exactly how he wished he could comfort her with a slow, deep kiss.

"Good night, Gus," she whispered. "See you in the morning."

"Good night, Tilda Mae."

He had almost closed the door when a thought occurred to him. "Actually, just remembered, I'm off from work tomorrow. Do ye think ye could get Amber to take yer shift?"

Till glanced at him sideways, her curiosity piqued. "I'm sure I could. She's been asking for extra hours. Why?"

"Well, I've got the odd list of one-offs to work tomorrow durin' the day. A rare occurrence, but when ye get them they're a lot of fun. I thought maybe comin' along would do ye some good."

"One-offs?"

"One time Fairy Godmother encounters, in which the person on the receiving end of the magic doesn't realize that they've met anyone more than a good Samaritan."

"Sounds interesting..." The thought crossed her mind that the idea of a day spent with Gus was a lot more appealing than the day of paperwork that awaited her at the store. "Thanks, I'd love to go."

He nodded and closed the door. He was certain Amber would take her shift, just as certain as he was that Till had no idea yet that she was going to have the time of her life.

Chapter Six

One-offs

TILL WAS WEARING A BEAUTIFUL LITTLE FLORAL DRESS that fell just to her knees, a white cardigan, and the ever-present pink high-tops when Gus met her at her door the next morning.

"Coffee?" she asked, motioning for him to come in.

"Sure, time for one." He took his usual spot at the kitchen table. He noticed that Till never sat in the chair that Aunt Tilda used to use... neither did he. No one ever did. In some ways, it still was her chair. Gus could feel her presence here the strongest of any place, and it assured him that at least somewhere out there, everything was just as it was supposed to be.

"I'm surprised to see you this morning," Till said, filling his cup the old fashioned way and pouring in a portion of cream. "I'm not looking forward to the backlog of work waiting for me at the store."

"At the store?" Gus frowned. "I thought ye were comin' with me today? What happened, couldn't Amber take yer shift?"

Till's expression altered, becoming one of dismay. "What are you talking about?"

Gus sensed no playfulness or deception in her; she was entirely serious. "Don't ye remember, Tilda Mae? We have *plans* today..." He waited to see if she would remember now, but confusion still reigned.

"I'm sorry, we had plans? I...oh, wait." She shook her head and then took a halting step forward. "Wait, don't tell me..." She inhaled sharply, seeming disoriented. "We were going to do something today. Something you said didn't happen often."

"That's right."

"*Is* Amber taking my shift? I wonder." She pulled the phone out of her pocket and dialed. "Amber? Yeah, it's Till… oh, don't worry about it, I really do have something else I need to do today. Yeah, the hours are yours. I'll see you later. Thanks again. Bye." She looked truly bewildered. "She's already on her way to the store. Odd that I'd forget like that."

"Yeah… odd." He frowned. "Are ye feelin' all right?"

"Fine," Till insisted, waving away his concern as she drank the rest of her coffee, then headed for the coat rack to retrieve her raincoat. "One-offs, I remember now. So let's go, tell me all about what we're supposed to do. In fact, you better tell me what I'm *not* supposed to do, if anything." She watched Gus drain his cup and set it back down. "Apparently I'm not firing on all thrusters today."

"Don't worry," Gus said, though he did worry. "I've always got yer back."

* * *

They headed to the Park and Ride lot in Gus's truck. Till smiled wistfully.

"Reminds me of all the times you took me to the university." She tugged gently at the pendant on the chain around her neck; the key Gus had given her for Christmas. He never saw her without it, and was comforted by the fact it meant so much to her. "Lots of good memories."

"Aye," Gus replied softly, as he put the truck in park. He could hardly stand the way she was looking at him now; with such a conflicting mixture of hesitation and affection in her eyes. Again, her thoughts went blank from his perspective. It was disorienting when it happened so suddenly, as though someone erased a blackboard you were reading; leaving nothing behind but chalk dust and the distinct impression you missed seeing something you needed to know for the test.

The uneasy moment of silence faded away, and afterward Gus could again sense the humming whirr of her mind spinning along. It was always a comfort to him.

"So what do we do now?" she asked.

"Now? We get to work," Gus said, giving her a slight smile. "I hope y'er up for a lot of transportin' today, because y'er gonna have to hold my hand to be able to keep up." He exited the truck and walked around, opening her door as was his custom. He reached up toward her. "Ready?"

She took hold of his outstretched hand. "As I will ever be."

"Right, then. Keep yer eyes open and follow my lead. Stay in my head, follow my thoughts, and ye'll know just what to do when the time comes."

"Got it."

"Remember the most important part of a one-off," he said, unable to stop himself from giving her fingers a gentle squeeze. "Be ready to make a quick getaway."

* * *

The pair appeared behind a tree in a small park, just a few feet away from a bustling intersection.

"First one's a bit tricky," Gus warned, finally releasing her hand. "Stay put and watch, yeah?"

"Aye," she said, giving him a quick salute. Before she could say anything more, he took off at a full run, racing toward the crosswalk.

A girl of about fourteen was crossing the street. She had the right of way, but her eyes were not on what she was doing; they were focused on the screen of her phone.

The sound and feel of air rushing by caught Till's attention as a car ran the red light. It barreled toward the girl at full speed.

"Look out!" Gus shouted. He swept the girl up into his arms and moved her out of the way at the very last second.

Cars screeched to a halt all around them as people reacted to the sight, causing a multi-car fender bender. It became clear that none of the drivers were hurt, as they all rushed from their vehicles to survey the damage.

Till watched as Gus whispered something into the young girl's ear. She nodded, still stunned, and then a moment later Gus was back at Till's side. He was gasping for air as he took her hand but managed to speak two words.

"Let's go."

* * *

He transported them to the deserted stockroom of a small grocery store. "I think ye can handle this next one," he said, as he still fought to catch his breath.

"You just saved that girl's life," she whispered, still trying to believe what she'd seen.

"Just doin' the job," Gus said. "We don't always get to win, Till, so have to appreciate the times we do."

She nodded.

"On with ye, then. Before the stock boy finds us back here." Gus nudged her forward, and they walked through the store, up toward the checkout stands.

Till fidgeted, bouncing up and down a little. "What do I do?"

"Just pay attention. Ye'll know."

She observed those around her with great concentration. There was an older man waiting in line to buy a pie and half gallon of ice cream. A woman with a basket full of fresh vegetables stood behind him.

In the next lane over was an exhausted looking young woman, struggling with a crying baby and a hand-basket that contained formula and diapers.

As Till and Gus observed her, it became clear to him that the woman was more than a little nervous. She watched the total add up on her order and appeared defeated.

"Nineteen dollars," the cashier said, pausing to pop her bubblegum, "and seventy-six cents."

The young mother began rifling around first in her wallet, then her diaper bag, and then her pockets. "No…oh no…" she mumbled, panicking.

Till picked up a pack of gum from the display beside her and then hopped into line behind the woman.

Gus looked away, grinning as he pretended to leaf through a magazine from the rack. She had this, no problem.

"Something wrong?" the cashier asked, sighing with irritation.

"I had five dollars more, I'm sure of it." A tremor rattled the young woman's voice. "I know it's here somewhere…" After another moment of unsuccessful searching, tears filled her eyes. She regarded the items on the counter, clearly wondering how she was going to decide between the formula and the diapers if she couldn't pay for both.

"Did you say you lost five dollars?" Till piped up, and the woman nodded. "Isn't that weird? I found this in my coat pocket this morning, had no idea it was there. Must have gone through the wash ten times." Till pulled out a crumpled twenty dollar bill and held it out toward the cashier.

The woman shook her head profusely. "Oh no, I couldn't let you..."

"Please," Till said, handing the money over. "It would be my pleasure." Before the woman knew what had happened, Till had paid for her order and the cashier began to ring up Till's pack of gum.

"I... don't know how to thank you..." The woman extended her hand, and Till pressed something into it as she shook it.

"I know how you can thank me. Why don't you take yourself and the little one out for a nice lunch."

The baby began to squirm fiercely in her mother's arms, giving Till and Gus just the moment of distraction they needed to head for the parking lot and then vanish.

When they arrived at their next location, Gus smiled his approval. "She won't know what to do with that fifty dollar bill ye left her with," he said proudly. "Above and beyond, Till. Anymore and she'd have been uncomfortable, but today ye made her feel like she won the lottery. You restored her faith in humanity, just a little bit. Even if it took magic to do it, that's what one-offs are all about. They're about teachin' people there is still somethin' left to believe in."

"I think it reminds me, too," Till replied. "There really is so much for us to do."

* * *

After spending the rest of their day in multiple, small acts of kindness (which included, at one point, actually rescuing a kitten from a tree) the tired pair returned to the Park and Ride lot, then headed home in Gus's truck.

Till smiled at him as she walked up the front steps. "Thank you, I really needed today more than I can explain."

"Was happy to have ye along. Now ye better get a little rest... mornin' comes again before ye know it and we'll be due at the store. Big day tomorrow."

He was speaking of the bookstore's anniversary party.

"Don't I know it. Mom's been planning this event for months. I'd better go in early to be sure everything is ready."

"Suppose I'll join ye."

Till's tired smile turned to a grin. "Coffee later?"

Gus grinned, too, as his heart beat once again out of cadence at the sight of her. "Wouldn't miss it for the world."

Chapter Seven

May I Have This Dance?

THE PARTY MARKING THE CENTURY POINT since Happily Ever After Books had opened was to be a grand event, with games, catering, and of course, stories read aloud.

Gus was, at the moment, quite amused by Till as she made herself dizzy blowing up balloons. Even more amused than by the happy children who received the animals she turned those balloons into.

If I didn't have my powers, the only balloon animal I'd be able to make would be a snake, she thought to him, and he laughed.

"Something funny, Gus?" Mrs. Nesbitt asked, curious because she was not in on the joke he had heard in his mind.

"Just admirin' yer daughter's talent with the wee ones," Gus said.

"I'd suggest you give the balloons a try, but I was wondering, would you do the next storybook reading? It's scheduled to start in three minutes."

Till was now the one snickering. She and Gus both knew that her mother was only asking because she was so enamored of his accent.

I'm convinced she sometimes asks you questions just to hear you answer, Till thought, and color rose to Gus's face.

"Well, then," he said to Mrs. Nesbitt, clearing his throat, "If that would please ye, Missus, I would be happy to." He pretended to tip an imaginary cap to her, and she giggled like a school girl in the way that always made Till cringe.

"I knew I could count on you. Thanks, Gus."

She has a wee bit of a crush on you, Till thought next, but before Gus could think something back to her, he once again experienced the unsettling sensation of her mind going blank to him.

He laughed nervously now, and bowed slightly to his employer. "I'd… better get a move on, if I am goin' to do that readin'."

"The book is over in the story corner. It's a fairy tale collection. Take your pick!"

"I think we'll stick to the classics," Gus glanced over at Till and raised a brow. "Cinderella, perhaps?"

After the last child had a balloon to his liking, Till made her way over to the story corner, too. "I can't *wait* to hear this." She stood off to the side, her lips curling into a smirk. She watched as Gus tried his best to fit into the small chair meant for her mother, the usual story time reader. In the end he gave up trying and finally sat on the floor.

"Well, then," Gus began, addressing his small, eager audience… and their equally eager mothers. They had quite a group of regulars at the store, and many of them had taken a shine to Gus, just as Till's mother had. More than once he'd had to get himself out of a tricky situation with an enthusiastic local mom. He didn't like to talk about it, and Till never teased him about it, though she was, he noted, sorely tempted.

Gus opened the book and began to read the story of the young girl who toiled to care for the house while her stepmother and stepsisters lived in luxury. When the introduction of the Fairy Godmother took place he looked up, glanced across the room, and held Till's gaze for a second.

Twin circles of red appeared on her cheeks, which pleased him highly.

As he was reading, a young hand shot up into the air and began waving at him, endlessly. He nodded to the boy but the child had no intention of sitting there in silence. He had a question, and he expected an answer.

Finally, Gus was forced to stop reading. "Did ye have somethin' to say, young sir?"

"Well, I was just wondering," the boy asked thoughtfully, "why aren't the fairy people ever guys?"

Giggles arose from the crowd, but Gus nearly choked. "Sorry? What did ye say?"

"Why aren't there ever Fairy Godfathers?"

For once in his life, Gus had no idea what to say.

"Maybe that story just hasn't been written yet," Till said, jumping in to rescue him. "Maybe you'll be the one to write it!"

"I think I will," the little boy decided, nodding with certainty. "And you can sell it in the bookstore."

"Well, at least we can read it at story time!" Mrs. Nesbitt suggested, and turned to his mother as she added, "A young author *and* future entrepreneur! You must be very proud."

The mother nodded and motioned for the boy to be silent now.

Till listened with a wistful expression on her face as Gus continued the story. As the happy ending approached, he looked up and noticed she was nowhere to be seen. He reached out for her thoughts, and found they were still beyond his ability to access.

Afterward he finally caught up with her over by the refreshment table, where the children had gathered and were enjoying cake and punch.

Till had some punch but made a special effort, Gus noticed, to avoid the chocolate cake. Clearly she had learned her lesson when it came to indulging in that substance, which was so intoxicating to Fairy Godparents.

A little girl named Allison tugged at Till's sleeve to get her attention. Till had known Allison's mother in high school, and the girl had been visiting the store since she was a newborn. "I wish I knew how to do the wal… wal… what was that dance Cinderella did at the ball?"

"The waltz?" Mrs. Nesbitt replied, sweeping in and holding out a plate of cookies toward the children, guaranteeing they would be on a sugar rush the rest of the day.

"Yeah!" Allison said. She turned bright and shining eyes up toward Gus. "Do you know how to waltz dance, Gus?"

"I happen to know that he does," Till volunteered, unable to hide her amusement as she made a suggestion. "Maybe he'll give you a lesson."

"Oh! Would you, please? Please, Gus, please?" Allison begged.

Half the women in the store seemed to lean forward and stare at Gus, looking as though they wished he would give *them* a lesson instead.

Gus blushed deeply. "I don't know, Miss Allison… I'm a bit tall for ye…"

"Then you can demonstrate with another partner!" Mrs. Nesbitt suggested, clapping her hands together. Gus heard a thought as it screamed loud and clear through Till's mind:

Dear God, please do not let my mother volunteer.

"Yes, I suppose I could," Gus decided, taking control of the situation.

Oh no, you don't... Till thought next, but it was too late. The words had already left his lips and been heard by everyone present.

"Maybe Miss Till will help me out?" He glanced at her almost shyly now. He took great care to guard his emotions; forcing to the forefront of his mind the fact that they had danced together before, when she was just learning at the university.

Sensing her reluctance, he took a step forward and widened his eyes, almost issuing the invitation as a challenge.

I think ye owe me one by now, he thought.

"Darn!" Till said, snapping her fingers as though disappointed. "We don't have any waltzing music!" Her expression said she thought she'd won, but her mother was not about to let this opportunity pass.

"I'll fix *that*!" Mrs. Nesbitt rushed behind the front counter. She slapped a cassette into the store's antiquated stereo system and pressed play. "Might be a little fast for a waltz, but I think you two will figure it out. Stand back, everyone. Make some room!"

The group did as told, and Gus could feel a distinct change in the atmosphere. Several of the women were now intensely jealous of Till.

The sound of a turn-of-the-twentieth-century-style orchestra filled the air, and Gus approached Till slowly. The crowd stood motionless, even the children, focused on their every move as Gus reached out a hand and extended it to her.

His voice was now a low rumble that only Till could hear as he spoke tenderly into her ear. "May I have this dance?"

"Thank you," she answered, lowering her eyes.

Just like I taught ye, Tilda Mae... he thought.

I'll try not to break your toes.

Big boots, remember? I can take it.

One of his hands grasped hers, the other took up position at her waist. Till's free hand held out the skirt of her dress as if it were a gown.

Grand, Tilda Mae. Just grand.

They spun around, dancing in a small circle, and for an instant, Gus sensed an affectionate, resonant warmth in her that he remembered all too well. It lasted for only a second before her thoughts became distant, muddled, and impossible to read.

The song ended with the older ladies in the store singing along with the final chorus, and when they finished, Gus twirled Till once before stopping and bowing at the waist before her. Applause filled the room, and Mrs. Nesbitt rushed up to him and took hold of him by the arms.

"I *knew* you'd be a wonderful dancer, Gus! Didn't you, Till?" When Till didn't answer, both of them looked around.

"Till?" Gus called, but she was nowhere to be seen.

"I think she went in the back," Allison's mother said, pointing in that direction. Gus tried to make his way through the throngs of his admirers to get to Till, but it was impossible.

When he did finally catch up to her, he observed that her eyes were red and swollen. Her mind was once again hidden behind a wall that felt like it was made of stone; her thoughts locked up tight.

"Ye've been cryin', Tilda Mae?" he whispered, glancing quickly back over his shoulder with the knowledge he only had a moment before her mother was going to drag him off to talk with more of their customers.

"No. Of course not." She gazed up at him and sniffled softly. "Allergies."

He looked at her sideways, and, though he decided not to pry, he knew she was being entirely untruthful.

* * *

The anniversary celebration had been an enormous success, but one that left Till's parents more exhausted than Gus could ever remember seeing them. Till was worried, too, and she exchanged a glance with Gus that said it all. They needed to take care of cleaning up the store tonight.

"Mom, why don't you two go on home, Gus and I can take care of all of this. Right, Gus?"

"Of course, would be happy to."

"Oh, we couldn't think of it," Mrs. Nesbitt objected.

"Don't worry about a thing," Till assured.

"But what about Annabelle?" Mrs. Nesbitt asked, referring to the cat that Gus had given her last Christmas. "Poor thing, she was skittish all day, with so many children around. She's gone into hiding. I can't get her to come out so we can take her home."

"Don't worry, Missus," Gus said, holding open her coat so she could put it on. "We'll see Annabelle home after everything is put right."

"Oh... all right, then. Her carrier is in the back." Mrs. Nesbitt finally acquiesced. She sighed and smiled. "Thank you, both of you. Things did go pretty well today, didn't they?" She buttoned up her coat as her husband held the door open for her. "It was lovely. The dancing part, especially."

Till's lips curled up in a small smile that quickly faded, the moment she heard her mother's last words, muffled though they were, from the other side of the glass door. *"If only Till didn't have two left feet."*

"She always does that," Till muttered.

"Does what?" Gus asked, though he had a pretty good idea what she meant.

"That... thing she does. She can never say something nice without putting that little dig in at the end. It gets to me."

"Has it always been this way?"

"Long as I can remember, even when I was little." She shrugged, and Gus felt a sudden chill as she was haunted by some memory or other he could not access. "I love my mother, but I mean..." She stopped and waved her hand, trying, it seemed, to sweep the feelings away in mid-air. "I don't know. I'm probably just being overly sensitive. She always said I was. Maybe all mothers are like that."

"No," Gus replied softly. He gestured slightly with one hand, using his powers to straighten the books on the shelf before him and magically rearranging the titles that were out of order. "Not all mothers are like that."

"Just once in my life, I'd like to do something, *anything*, that pleased her completely," Till remarked, leaning back against the wall and looking up at the ceiling. "Whatever it might be. The closest I've ever come was, well..."

"Go on."

Till reddened. "Bringing you to work here."

Gus reddened, too. "That can't be."

"Oh, trust me, it's true. Still, at the end of the whole process of hiring you and seeing how perfectly you fit here, she did scold me for not asking you to consider working here sooner." She sighed. "Again, that little criticism. Always."

"In the end, Tilda Mae, ye know she loves ye. She wants ye to be happy."

"You're taking her side?" Till took up a defensive posture. "I don't believe this."

Warning bells rang in Gus's head, but he was in too deep now to try to back out gracefully. "That's not what I meant. What I meant was—"

"Oh, I know what you meant," Till snapped, turning away. "You meant that I *am* being overly sensitive, just like she always says."

"I meant no such thing, Tilda Mae, if ye'd only listen."

"I don't need to listen to any more of this. You think she's so perfect, you think that if I just listened to her and acted the way she wants that things would be a lot smoother between us."

"That's not what I'm thinkin' at all!" Gus insisted, ducking around her to force himself into her line of vision. "Y'er readin' me all wrong. I didn't mean anythin' by any of it, just that I'm sorry she's ever made ye feel less than what ye are."

"And what am I?" Till pressed, her voice quivering.

Perfect, Gus thought, but he forced the thought down, and prayed to any powers that may be that she didn't pick up on it. "Ye are exactly what ye should be," he said, leaning down to try to catch her gaze as she lowered her eyes to the floor. "Ye are a daughter with y'er own free will. Ye show me a single mother that has ever really been okay with *that*. I wish…" He stopped, unsure if he should continue.

"What?"

He paused, considering, before finally going on. "I wish that ye could hear the way she talks about ye when y'er not around."

Till shifted again, her posture relaxing slightly. "What do you mean?"

"When she speaks of ye to others. She never has anything but the kindest words to say. Her daughter Till, who graduated top of her class. Her daughter Till, who practically runs the bookshop now that her parents are gettin' on in years. It's 'Till this, and Till that'…" He could tell she was having a hard time believing him, but Gus was entirely sincere. "She worships the ground ye walk on, Tilda Mae. Believe it."

"I wish I could."

The sound of a jingling bell was heard, and Gus soon felt something soft and warm brush against his leg. It was the elusive Annabelle, finally out of hiding.

He was right when he suspected the cat would end up coming to the store during the days. She didn't seem to mind the ride in the car, Mrs. Nesbitt said, and the woman couldn't bear the thought of leaving the cat home alone all day. Today had all been a bit much for the little thing, though, and Gus felt sorry for her.

It had been a bit much for them all.

"Hello, there, Annabelle." He reached down and stroked his fingers through the cat's silky fur. "You return at last. Water bowl empty again, or are ye anglin' for one of those treats the Missus keeps in her desk? Hmm?"

Watching him with the cat, Till's expression softened and her body began to relax even more. He knew that the separation she felt from her mother was very real, but he wished she could see that it wasn't as bad as she imagined it to be.

"Why don't ye try givin' a meow to Miss Till over there?" he suggested to Annabelle. "I hear she's a soft touch where y'er concerned."

"Me?" Till gave a little laugh. "If you have your way, that cat is going to weight twenty pounds because of all the treats you give her. Don't let me get in the way of that beautiful arrangement."

"Very well," Gus said, turning toward the stockroom with the cat just a half-step behind him. He paused. "Till, I mean it. If ye could only hear what she says, ye'd feel a lot better."

"Maybe someday she'll think to tell me some of those good things. Without additional commentary."

"I hope so." Gus sighed, and then left Till alone to her thoughts as he sought out the cat's promised treat.

Chapter Eight

Someone New

THE SHELVES AT HAPPILY EVER AFTER BOOKS were sparsely populated: picked over from all the extra sales during the celebration the day before.

Lost in thought, Gus was busy restocking when he caught the aroma of fresh coffee in the air. Till approached with a cup in hand. She looked weary, and he wished that she could have taken a few days off after the event. But things had picked up lately at the store, to the point where they were steadily busy again, and so neither of them had an easy time calling in whether they felt up to working or not.

"What's up?" he asked, knowing that she wouldn't just stand around unless she had something to ask. She handed him the cup. "For me? Very kind of ye, but it's not break time yet."

"Yes it is," Till said, motioning for him to follow her to the stockroom.

He tried to get a read on what she was thinking, but even under the most mundane conditions, it was becoming increasingly difficult. She had gained quite a mastery over her thoughts. They were nowhere near as obvious to him as they once had been, though the look on her face was almost as telling most of the time. She was nervous about something, that much was clear, whether he could read her mind in the moment or not.

"I'm getting a new one," she whispered, once she was sure they were alone.

Gus's eyebrows shot heavenward. "Charge?" he whispered back. "So soon?"

"Yeah." She bit her lip for a moment before continuing. "She's supposed to be about seven years old. I don't know the whole story yet, but I'm to meet her through the children's hospital volunteer program."

God, no, Gus thought. *Tell me they didn't give her one she's going to have to nurse through the transition... especially not one so young.*

"She's not terminal— at least, I don't believe she is," Till answered his thought without hesitation. Her 'reading' skills had also improved exponentially... and it left him disoriented when she could read him but he couldn't do the same in return. "I'm not sure yet. They didn't give me a lot of details."

"Tryin' to see what ye can figure out on yer own," he said. "That's the next step. Sometimes they give ye a charge and no information whatsoever. Better to start this way, I guess." He gave her a gentle, half-smile before he took a sip of his coffee and nodded his thanks for it. "I'm proud of ye, Till."

"Will you go with me tonight?" Till wrung her hands as she awaited his answer. Even though he'd never turned her down before, if he was at all able to do what she asked. "Even if she can't see you right away, just to know you're there would really help me a lot."

The tremor in her voice tugged at Gus's heart. It was a reminder of how even the smallest things about her could render him defenseless. "Of course, I will."

"Till! I need help out here!" Mrs. Nesbitt called from the front, and Till turned on her heel with a quick thought of thanks, sent directly into Gus's mind from her own.

* * *

Hours later, Till stood before a mirror in the entryway at home and analyzed her appearance.

She was wearing all white beneath a red and white striped smock. She had been issued a nametag and hospital ID, identifying her as one of the volunteers.

"I'm too old to be a candy striper," she muttered.

"Y'er young to be anythin'," Gus replied, leaning against the door frame. "Any more insights into the identity of this little lady?"

"She's definitely a repeat patient at the hospital," Till said, anxiously twisting her hair into a bun and sticking two long, decorative hairpins into it. He recognized the ornaments; they had belonged to

Aunt Tilda. "I don't know much else. I guess I am supposed to go into this blind as a bat and hope I don't fly into a wall."

"Won't be so bad, I promise." Gus assured. "Ye'll be able to get a read on her, right away. Y'er good at this, Till. Remember that."

"I feel like it's my first night all over again."

"Always feels like that when ye get a new charge. It's completely normal."

"Me, completely normal." Till smirked. "*That* would be a first."

"We'd better get a move on if ye want to introduce yerself before visitin' hours are over."

"Right." Till adjusted her collar and nodded. "Let's go."

* * *

The disconcerting sight of people in pain, and the unsettling sounds that accompanied it, greeted Gus the moment they walked through the door.

The stench of bleach, perspiration, and anguish hung thick in the air, and the sense of dread Till felt coming into this place was multiplied a thousand fold because the people languishing inside were so small. It was so overwhelming that not only was it clear to Gus that Till was suffering before they even set foot inside, but she almost tripped over her own shoes as she moved through the revolving door.

He reached out to steady her by the shoulders. "Are ye going to make it?"

"I hope so," Till replied, sounding entirely unsure. "It depends upon which wing they assign me to."

"I need to make myself scarce," Gus said, since he was not signed up to join the volunteer program and tagging along wouldn't be allowed. "Promise, I won't be far away."

"I'm going to hold you to that," Till said. She drew a deep breath, squared her shoulders, and headed for the volunteer coordinator's office.

* * *

Gus ducked into the nearest men's room and emerged in full uniform... a disguise that would serve him well for the moment and allow him to keep close tabs on Till.

He followed a safe distance behind her, pushing a mop and bucket of water along with him, boarding the elevator next to hers and taking from her thoughts what he needed to be able to exit on the right floor. He reassured her as best he could with a single, continuous thought:

I'm right behind you.

The hospital was enormous, a maze and marvel of modern architecture. Its technology was unsurpassed in the region; still, far too many tragedies occurred here. Gus hoped with all his heart that one of those sad stories was not awaiting Till in room 4305 of the cardiac wing.

He attuned his thoughts as closely as he dared to Till's; allowing him to listen in as he absently ran the mop up and down the same strip of tile outside the designated room.

Through the window Gus could see the little girl in her bed, staring out the window, an expression in her eyes much too troubled to belong to someone so young.

"Hello!" Till said brightly, and Gus's heart skipped a beat. She really did bring the sun with her into any room she entered, no matter how dark the place that contained it.

"Hello," the little girl replied cautiously. She pulled her thin cotton blanket up to her chin, which made her look even smaller.

"My name is Till, and I work here," Till pushed a small cart filled with books and other amusements before her. "What's your name?" Even as she asked the question, the name *Emma* crossed her mind, and Gus's.

"Emma," the little girl said, nodding weakly.

"Would you like something from my cart, Emma?" Till asked. "Something to help make the time go by faster?"

"They said I can't share the books, they're too germy," Emma replied sadly. "Same with the toys. The other kids are allowed to play with them, but I'm not."

"Oh, I see." Gus's mind filled with new thoughts as Till turned her own toward the little girl's and began to gather information. Of course the information she could gather was at a seven-year-old level; so she could only understand, in this moment, the situation as well as the child who was living it.

Gus felt her heart sink, and wished he could buoy her strength somehow.

I'm right out here... he thought to her again, and he saw her glance up toward the doorway. She caught sight of him in his janitorial overalls, and a genuine smile spread across her lips. She gave her head a slight shake as she thought back to him.

You never cease to amaze me.

Gus smiled too; and he glanced back down at the floor as he remembered he ought to keep mopping. He moved a little ways down the hall, then back again as he continued to listen in.

"Well, it so happens that I have some brand *new* books with me today," Till said, rummaging through the contents of the cart. "What kind would you like? Maybe I have something close."

The little girl sighed heavily. "I really wish I had some crayons," she said, staring out the window again. "And a coloring book."

Till's reaction was profound, and a lump rose in Gus's throat that matched the one in hers. Here this child was, stuck in the hospital in such serious condition, and all she wanted was something to draw with. He glanced up to see what Till would do next.

Till turned her back to the girl, pretending to be searching her cart. "Well, what do you know?" she said a moment later, holding up a box of crayons and a coloring book she had just covertly conjured into existence.

"Ponies! My favorite!" Emma gasped, her hands quickly emerging from beneath the blanket. She stopped, unsure whether she should reach out for the items Till displayed.

"They're yours, then," Till said, setting them down at the foot of the bed.

"Thank you so much!"

"You're welcome." Gus sensed that Till hated to go, but thought that if the child was being so carefully kept away from potential exposure to germs, that she had better not be seen in the room for long without explicit permission of someone on staff. "It was nice to meet you, Emma. I'll see you again later."

"Oh, you have to go?" Emma's face fell. "Okay. Bye." She fingered the crayons in the box but now seemed reluctant to use them.

"Bye…" Till moved through the doorway, but still didn't want to leave. Another thought crossed her mind, and she smiled.

Atta girl, Gus thought. *See what you can find out…*

A frantic nurse came rushing toward her. "Who are you? What were you doing in that room? Didn't you see the notes on the whiteboard? She can't share the toys with the other children, she's due for surgery soon and the risk is too great!"

"The crayons and book are brand new, I swear…" Till stammered, turning red.

"How do you know? What is this, your first night on the job? I've never seen you before." The woman clamped her hands down on her hips. "You've got a lot to learn…"

Before Till could speak again, another nurse, this one with a familiar face, approached; ready to diffuse the situation as only she could.

"Is there a problem?" Dianne asked, placing herself between Till and the first nurse.

"Oh, Dianne," the woman huffed. "This girl just gave Emma Hudson a coloring book and box of crayons. I was about to explain to her how important it is that Emma not be exposed to any preventable risks. She's new here. She doesn't know what she's…"

Gus kept listening in, sweeping by with his mop, whistling a little, giving Dianne and Till a glance before he moved on down the hall. Dianne would have the situation well in hand momentarily, of that Gus had no doubt.

"She's new, but she knows what she's doing," Dianne insisted.

"How do you know?"

"Because I know her. She's my landlord. That's how she was referred to volunteer here, I recruited her myself."

Till's eyes questioned if this was true, and sensed from Dianne's thoughts that it actually was. Dianne was the one who had suggested Till as a match to be Emma's Fairy Godmother.

"Oh, I… didn't know."

"I know you didn't, Sybil," Dianne replied. "Why don't you let me remind Till of the importance of being careful around Emma, and then you can get back to your patients."

Sybil nodded and, without acknowledging Till again, rushed off.

"Sorry about that," Dianne said, looking up at Till. "She doesn't like volunteers." She turned slightly and raised an eyebrow at Gus as he once again swept past with the mop. "Or janitors."

Gus laughed softly, and started to whistle again as he kept right on mopping.

"So you're the reason I'm here?" Till asked, wringing her hands. "I'm terrified to go near the girl now."

"Don't be. Just don't come near her if you even *think* you're coming down with a cold, and only bring her new things," Dianne said, loud enough for others to hear and purely for show. Emma had taken note of the ruckus in the hall and was staring curiously at them. She waved and Dianne quickly waved back; then lowered her voice before continuing. "She's so lonely, that one. Her parents are stuck at home most of the time with baby twins. They're torn, they want to be here but they really can't as much as Emma needs them to."

"So I'm here," Till answered.

"So you're here," Dianne concluded. "Don't be in such a hurry to run off, why don't you stay with her a little while?"

"Would it be okay?"

"Glove up, put on a mask…" She now thought to Till instead of speaking aloud. *Your powers will protect her from any real risk from you, don't worry. Just for appearances. If anyone gives you any trouble, send them to me. Don't stay more than half an hour.*

Till nodded.

One more thing, don't appear to be too friendly with the janitor. Dianne added. *He looks like trouble.*

Till blushed, and Gus, for his part, just kept whistling when Dianne added *I know you can hear me, Angus Duncan.*

Till watched as Dianne reached into a bin on the wall and pulled out a mask and pair of gloves. "Here you are," she said. "Now, go see if you can get a smile out of that child, will you? We've been trying for days, to no avail."

"Dianne, she's… she's not going to…" Till could barely bring herself to think the thought, and Dianne shook her head.

"No, she's not."

Till's shoulders visibly relaxed, and the smile returned to her face. As long as little Emma wasn't expected to die, she believed that she could handle this.

She knocked on the door with one bare hand before pulling her second glove on.

"Hi, it's me again. Till."

The little girl had resumed her staring out the window and did not look up. "I was wondering... could I color with you for a little while? It's been so long since I've been able to do it. Nurse Dianne said it would be okay."

Emma's face lit up. "Sure!" She scooted over on the bed to make room for Till, but Till shook her head.

"No, I better use the table. Here..." She pulled up a chair and wheeled the table over Emma's bed, closer to her. "This will work fine for me. I think I have some more crayons around here..." She patted the pockets of her smock and procured another box of crayons she'd just created.

"What about a coloring book?"

Till thought a moment and turned to her cart. She 'found' several sheets of blank white paper that had magically appeared among its contents. "I'm all set, the book is yours."

The little girl considered the bright box of crayons and looked at Till thoughtfully. "What colors are you gonna use?"

Till considered. "Black, blue, red, and yellow to start. Oh, and the peach. What about you?"

"Gray!" She held the crayon up on display, and then began to use it to fill in one of the horses in the coloring book. "I might get to go ride a real pony one day, after I'm better."

Till's heart caught in her throat and she barely looked up as Gus came into the room and began wiping down every visible surface with pungent, hospital-sanctioned disinfectant. "Do you mind if I ask what's wrong?" she inquired softly.

"My heart is broken," the little girl replied quickly, and honestly. "They have to fix it."

"I see," Till bit her lip, trying to stem a sudden flood of emotion. She cleared her throat and centered herself as Gus sent her that same comforting thought...

I'm right behind ye.

"They have to put in a pace... pace..."

"Pacemaker?"

"Yeah, that's it. Pacemaker. To fix my heart. Gonna do it soon, I think. They never tell me anything." She switched colors and began to fill in the horse's mane with a purple crayon. "I wish I had a purple horse. Don't you?"

"That would be fun..." Till replied, as she started to draw a little picture and kept glancing up at Emma as she worked.

"So when they fix my heart, it won't be broken anymore," Emma said. "I will be able to do a lot more things. I wish they would tell me what, but they said we have to wait and see."

Gus tried to imagine how difficult going through a process like this would be for a child Emma's age, especially without an extreme amount of support from her parents. No wonder Till was recruited to visit her. If there was ever a case for a Fairy Godparent, this was it.

"Have you ever had a broken heart?" Emma asked.

Gus stepped toward the door, lingering just enough as he pretended to wipe down the window to observe.

"Not broken like yours is," Till replied, and instantly her mind went blank to Gus again. He wondered just what she was going to say next. "Sometimes, it sure feels like it, though."

"When you're sad?" Emma asked, coloring away.

"Yeah," Till replied honestly. "When I'm sad."

Whatever ye've got to be broken hearted over, Tilda Mae, I wish I could fix it for ye... Gus thought, taking care to dismiss his feelings as quickly as possible, so as not to share them with anyone else.

"Well, when you get sad, you can look at this and maybe it will make you happy." Emma ripped her artwork from the book and handed it to Till. Tears glistened in Till's eyes as she observed the pony in the picture; gray and purple, with a gigantic smile drawn onto its face. She smiled gently.

"Thank you, Emma. When you get sad, maybe this will remind you that you'll be home soon." Till held up the picture she'd been drawing; a blue house, a mother and father outside and little Emma standing before two toe-headed infants.

Emma gasped. "How did you know my house is blue? And our car is red? That's my family!"

Till didn't have a non-magical answer to offer, so she just shrugged. "I'm a good guesser." She stood up, realizing that she had better not stay any longer on her first visit. She pinned the picture to the board on the wall where Emma could see it. "I enjoyed coloring with you, Emma. Good luck with your operation."

"Will you come to see me again?" the child pleaded. "I wish you could come see me after I was out of the hospital."

"I can't make any promises," Till said, though Gus picked up on the fact that she was already brainstorming ways in which to make that work. "But I'll try."

"Thank you for coloring with me."

"You're welcome." Till tucked her crayons back into her pocket. The child was beginning to nod off, so Till set her prizes on the table and wheeled it back beside the bed. "Sweet dreams, little Emma. I will see you again, before you know it."

Gus discreetly made his exit now. He stepped into an empty elevator, transferred himself back into his street clothes, and waited for Till outside the entrance to the hospital.

The look on his face when he saw her was one of complete wonder.

"What?" she asked, as she inevitably did whenever he stared at her a moment too long.

He responded slowly. "Ye just never cease to amaze *me*."

Chapter Nine

Darkness Will Fall

"WHAT A NIGHT," TILL SAID, as she unlocked the front door and moved slowly through it. She held tightly to the drawing Emma had given her. "This goes on the fridge." She smiled up at Gus. "Want something to eat?"

Gus couldn't speak; in this moment, his heart was too full. She was so lovely, so close, and he wished so much that he could give her a kiss good night. He fought to block the thought, and doing so made him feel weary. It was exhausting, being so careful what he thought around her.

"No thank ye, Tilda Mae. Think I will just have a bit of a lie down."

"You feeling all right, or do I need to worry?"

"No need," he promised, though the truth was that he was worried, himself. What if she picked up on the stray, momentary thought he just couldn't hide? Fortunately, she seemed too lost in her own head tonight to notice his frame of mind.

"Okay, then. Rest well."

"See ye in a few hours."

"Coffee?"

"Sure thing. Good night." Gus turned and was about to round the corner toward the renter's entrance to the house when he sensed another presence nearby. He stopped where he stood. It was Lane, and he was not going to visit Till for social purposes.

He started to turn around, to go back, but then reminded himself it was none of his business what Lane wanted to discuss with Till. He hesitated, trying to move forward, but seemed unable to get his boots free of the sidewalk. He was still close enough to hear their voices without resorting to using his skills to listen in, and decided that for the moment it was better to stay put, just to get an idea of what Lane wanted.

"Tilly," Lane began, and Gus knew Till would cringe.

"Don't call me that," she snapped. "What do you want, Lane? I'm tired."

"Is that *all* you are, Tilda Mae?"

"Only one person gets to call me *that*." Anger rose in her voice to a greater degree than mere annoyance now. "And that's *not* you."

"Familiar, aren't you, with the Leprechaun these days? One might wonder just how familiar."

Gus wanted to turn around right now and stop Lane's line of questioning, but he was torn. He knew how much more 'familiar' he and Till had really been. No one else did, not even she remembered; and that was the way that it had to stay. If he interfered now, it may become too clear, and the consequences would be catastrophic.

Till stood her ground. "Again, I'm going to ask you what you want, Lane?"

"I want you to come with me to the university for a little while," Lane said. "Chat with some on the board of governors who have been watching your progress. They are keeping a very close eye on you, Tilly. Much closer than they would on a regular first-year post grad. I keep trying to figure out why."

"Well, maybe the reason you can't figure it out is because it's none of your business."

Lane laughed in a way that sent a chill through Gus. "I'm an advisor to the board; of course your performance is my business. Especially since I'm one of those who objected to you being paired with the Celtic wonder to begin with."

Color rose in Gus's face. He was about to intervene when Till unknowingly reminded him that she could take pretty good care of herself.

"Unless I receive some kind of official summons or directive to appear before the board for any reason, you can stuff it, Lane. I have no intention of being a guinea pig for your personal brand of research."

Now Lane's laugh sounded truly twisted — unlike Gus had ever heard. "Ironic that you use that word, Tilda Mae. You are something of an experiment, aren't you? Oh well. I suppose I just have to be patient…" He lowered his voice and Gus strained to hear. He finally resorted to reading Lane's thoughts, which were as clear as they were frightening. *The cracks will begin to show, little girl, when you break under pressure. Darkness will fall on you, and no one will be able to save you from yourself.*

Gus felt Till's mood shift, and he wanted nothing more than to return to her side, to immediately comfort her. He knew he couldn't, though; if he tried, it would only complicate whatever it was that had her so upset.

Could she really still be so nervous about the fact that Lane disapproved of their pairing, or was more going on than Gus could read?

She said nothing more before slamming the door behind her.

Worse than the physical barrier closing between them was the fact that Till's very active mind was again blank to Gus— her thoughts completely beyond his ability to reach.

"What's goin' on with ye, Tilda Mae," he muttered, and as he looked up and prepared to take a step forward he found someone in his path who seemed perfectly willing to tell him.

"She's hiding something," Lane informed Gus, and Gus immediately stood taller with his chest out and his head held high.

"How are her thoughts any of yer business, old man?" Gus knew that Lane hated to be reminded of his age, and while he rarely dropped to such a level as to insult anyone, this time he couldn't stop himself.

"They are if they hint that she's more invested in your relationship than she should be," Lane replied. "The moment that we catch the hint of the 'f' word in the air..." He widened his eyes, emphasizing, "*fraternization*... I will shut your partnership down faster than you can say Fairy Godmother."

Gus's voice dropped. "Step off, Lane, I'm warnin' ye. Leave Till alone. If ye cause her a moment's anguish, ye'll wish ye'd never been born." He leaned closer, impressing the point upon Lane that Till had someone watching over her.

"Ooooh, the Leprechaun is trying to intimidate me!" Lane mocked Gus, leaning toward him as well. "Could she finally be the chink in that perfectly polished armor of yours?"

"She's no weakness, and just ye mind that," Gus whispered. "If anythin', she makes me stronger, and that is a strength ye do not want to test the power of. *Ever.*"

"Oh, the test will come, and not by my hand," Lane warned as he turned away at last. "You two have made your bed. Sooner or later, you're going to give in and lie in it."

Gus grasped hold of the back of Lane's jacket and held fast. "Now hear this. What Till and I do is between us and those with more power than ye'll *ever* have."

Lane broke free, narrowing his eyes. "I saw it, you know. I saw the whole thing."

"Whole thing?" Gus was evasive on purpose; he didn't want to give Lane a single thing to work with.

"Her paper on fraternization. And what's more, I saw you returning to your apartment in the early hours of January first."

"So ye really don't have anything better to do with yer life than spy on other people?" Gus reddened; not because he was embarrassed about what he and Till had done, but unhappy that Lane had put two and two together and come up with four. "As ye know, the fulfillment of a Fairy's One Wish is nobody's business, Lane, least of all that of their housemates and former mentors."

"True. Unless it becomes apparent that the people involved are still at great risk of breaking the code."

"What makes you think that—"

"Please. Do you think I'm an idiot?" Lane shook his head. "I know your wish has been fulfilled. I know it involved Till. I just don't know what Till might wish for, and I will be keeping my eyes on the both of you to be sure that nothing outside the boundaries of those wishes takes place."

"Such as?" Gus stepped closer, invading Lane's personal space with purpose.

"Such as... romantic involvement on a regular basis."

Gus wanted to throttle Lane and it took all of his reserve to hold back. He grasped hold of the front of Lane's jacket this time. "Ye'd better watch yer step, I warn ye…"

"Or what? You're hardly in a position to tell me what to do. As senior advisor to the board, I am untouchable. I can do what I want, when I want, and *no one* can stop me."

"So ye think," Gus warned. "Absolute power? Ye know what they say about that. And ye are absolutely corrupt. I wouldn't want to be in your place the day that the axe falls, and yer pride brings ye to a pitiful end."

"Is that a threat?"

"No such thing. Just a warnin' that I'll be watchin' ye as close as ye plan to watch us. And if a hair on Till's head is harmed because of ye, then ye will have to deal with me. I'm her partner, and I am still in the probationary mentoring period, during which I can use my powers to protect her with impunity. Don't think I won't do it."

"If you both behave yourselves then you'll have nothing to protect her from… or hasn't it occurred to you yet that the thing you most need to protect her from is herself?"

"I don't know what's happened to ye, Lane. Who ye've become, but it's not pretty. Ever since Aunt Tilda died—"

"Don't use her name in my presence," Lane barked. "You're not worthy of it."

"She thought I was plenty worthy to be her friend, and to look out for her great niece," Gus retorted. "What did she consider *ye* worthy of?"

"This conversation is over." Lane extricated himself from Gus's grasp and straightened his jacket. "You mark my words, Duncan, while my suffering may well be underway, yours is just *beginning*."

Gus remained where he was for a long time, contemplating what Lane had said. He almost sounded jealous whenever he referred to Gus and Till's partnership. Gus knew Lane well enough to know that he wasn't at all interested in Till romantically; so he was left with only one other question as he attempted to peer into Lane's thoughts, and found himself now blocked from even the most generic.

In answer to that question, a new thought crossed Gus's mind.

Could Lane be so determined to see them fail because he'd been denied a partnership he himself had wished for, centuries ago?

Chapter Ten
Morning

GUS CAME AROUND THE CORNER and up the walk to find Till waiting at the door.

Her smile was brighter than the day itself, and lit up his mind and heart. Her presence warmed him as nothing else could. He hurried to mask his thoughts, trying to focus on the first, absolutely random thing that entered his brain.

"As you wish," Till said aloud in response, as she closed the door behind him and gestured toward the table.

"Well, look at that." He laughed nervously. "Blueberry muffins."

"You were just thinking how much you'd like to have some with your coffee," Till said, with a satisfied grin. She bounced up and down with excitement. "I'm getting really good at that, aren't I? At reading you in a split second."

Too good, Gus thought.

Is there such a thing? Till thought back.

"Of course not," Gus hemmed, sitting down and picking up a muffin. "Y'er learnin' so fast, it just keeps me on my toes."

"That's what I live for." Till sat down and poured them both some coffee. "Going to be busy at the store today. I can't wait for it to be over, to get home tonight and put my feet up."

Gus took another bite and waited until he'd consumed it to continue. "I thought ye were due back at the hospital tonight?"

Till blinked, confused. "Hospital? Why would I be there?"

Gus laughed again, more nervously than before. "Very funny, Tilda Mae."

Till did not laugh. "No, seriously. What would I be doing at a hospital tonight?"

Gus's voice took on a tone of alarm. "Visiting Emma." He focused on her intently, and realized that she had no idea what he was talking about. This was the second time her memory had lapsed in recent days, and while once could have been a fluke, twice was truly frightening. "Till, are ye alright?"

"I'm fine," she insisted, "but who's Emma?"

The image of Emma flashed across Gus's mind. He projected the thought intentionally toward her, and the look on Till's face changed from one of bewilderment to one of recollection.

"Of course!" She shook her head, embarrassed. "Of course. Tomorrow morning is Emma's procedure, I have to be sure that I see her tonight beforehand."

Gus picked up his coffee and slowly drew from it, but swallowing did not clear away the lump in his throat. "Ye really worry me sometimes, Tilda Mae. Are you sure y'er feelin' all right?"

"Just a little tired this morning, that's all." She gave a broad, dismissive wave. "Coffee will fix me right up. Then we'll be off to work, and after work, on our way to Fairy Godparenting for the evening." She made light of the moment, but Gus sensed a nagging concern in her that he couldn't reconcile. "No wings, no wands, no waiting," she joked, but it fell flat. "That's the way we roll."

"Aye." He was going to have to keep an even closer eye on her until he found out why it was that she'd suddenly forgotten the Fairy Godmother part of her life... twice.

"Twice?" Till tried not to appear startled, but she was. Clearly she had no memory of the previous lapse.

"Till, is there anything I should know? Anything you're not telling me? Do you have any idea why you might be forgetting things this way?"

"I'm sure it's nothing," Till replied, tossing back the last of her coffee. Gus felt a distinct desire in her to move beyond the awkwardness of the moment. "C'mon, let's get going."

As much as she wanted to dismiss what had just happened, Gus knew that he wasn't going to be able to. It would bother him, until he got to the bottom of why it had happened in the first place at all, let alone a second time.

He could only hope and pray, in his fashion, that it didn't happen again.

Chapter Eleven
Mending Broken Hearts

ONCE AGAIN DISGUISED AS A JANITOR, Gus swished his mop up and down the bland, endless hospital floor tile. Till paced in the hall outside Emma's room, and he wished he could do something more to help her than just being near.

A doctor and nurse were in with Emma, and the curtains were closed. After what felt like forever, they were drawn open once more. Gus exchanged a look with Till as the medical staff emerged from the room and spoke frankly about Emma's family situation.

"I don't understand how they could do it," the nurse, Sybil, complained to the doctor. "I know they have other kids, but they always seem to be looking for any excuse they can come up with to get the hell out of here as fast as they can."

The doctor shook his head as the pair walked away. "If it was my child about to have heart surgery in the morning, nothing could make me leave. I'd find a way to make it work, somehow." He sighed. "People and their priorities in life. I will never understand them. I guess some people are not cut out to be parents."

Till shot Gus another look across the hall and then he lowered his eyes. Her thoughts raced through his mind as she contemplated the situation.

How do I ever begin to make up for absent parents?

Just do what you can, he thought back. *It's all we can ever do.*

Till drew a deep breath, grabbed a mask and pair of gloves from the bins on the wall outside of Emma's room, and went inside.

"Helloooo," she said in a bright, sing-song tone. "Anybody home?"

Gus couldn't help but smile at the sound of her voice. He could hear the quiver in it, though it would be undetectable to anyone who knew her less. He knew her so well, he could sense her fraying nerves through the butterflies in her stomach; which stirred up in a storm the moment she saw the look in Emma's eyes.

I'm never far away, Gus thought to her, noting her resolve as she finally continued on.

He positioned himself just outside the door again, listening as he mopped.

Emma remained silent.

"It's almost your big day, are you excited?" Till asked. "You're going to feel so much stronger after this is over. So much better. Just wait and see."

Emma offered no response.

"Hey," Till said softly, moving to the other side of the bed so she could see the girl's face, "you're shaking. Are you okay?"

Stupid question, idiot, Till immediately thought to herself.

Just keep talkin', Gus thought back. *No question is stupid in this instance*. He paused where he was and watched through the doorway.

"I'm afraid," Emma whispered, finally revealing her face to Till. "They said that they are going to make me go to sleep tomorrow for my operation. What if I don't wake up?"

"Of course you're going to wake up," Till assured, wishing she could reach out and physically comfort the child, but fearing there was no way to do it without drawing undue attention. "You won't be alone, Emma. All the doctors and nurses are going to be watching over you while you sleep, taking good care of you. Making you better. You just have to trust them."

"I wish my Mommy was here." Tears filled Emma's eyes, and Gus was almost overwhelmed by the emotions radiating from Till now. She wanted, for the first time, to say something she'd never said to anyone before; she wanted to explain who she really was, and what her purpose was in being there.

I need to tell her, Gus. She needs to know she won't be alone in all this, she thought, begging his permission without actually asking for it.

If ye think it best, Tilda Mae, tell her. He gave her a reassuring nod as she looked back at him. Then he took up his mopping again and moved down the hall, resuming use of his powers to listen in.

"Emma, I know you wish your mother was here, or your Dad. I do too, *believe me*." Irritation surfaced in Till's voice and she fought to smooth it over. "I would stay with you the whole time if I could so you wouldn't be alone. But you know what? I'm going to be watching over you, too. I promise."

"How can you watch over me if you're not here?" Emma asked, sniffling. "And after I go home, I won't ever see you again, will I, Till?"

"You'll see me," Till leaned just a little closer, trying to offer what physical comfort she could even if only by her proximity. "I promise."

"But you don't even know where I live, and besides, they might not let you come visit me. There might be rules."

"They can't really stop me..." Till drawled slowly, and Gus looked in again to see her rolling her eyes up toward the ceiling. After checking quickly to be sure no one else was within earshot, she continued. "Emma, I know we met here at the hospital but it wasn't just something that *happened*. It happened because it was *meant to happen*. And I promise as long as you need someone, you'll have me. You won't be alone."

"Are you my guardian angel?" Emma asked suddenly, sitting upright in bed. It was as though she understood something special was at work here, and she hung on Till's every breath as she waited for an answer.

"Not *quite*," Till whispered, moving closer. "But... have you ever heard of Fairy Godmothers?"

"Cinderella had one!" Emma exclaimed, growing excited. The rate on her heart monitor sped up and Till spoke softly, evenly, to try to calm her.

"Yes, that's how the story goes." Till motioned for the child to settle back down. "But it's not quite how it really works. You see, I am meant to be *your* Fairy Godmother, Emma, and I'll keep watch on you and show up to see you when you need me, or even sometimes when you least expect it."

"No one will believe me," Emma sighed, as she attempted to fold tiny arms crisscrossed by IVs and wires over her chest.

"Probably not, and I have to be careful that they don't see me when I come visit you outside the hospital. Adults, they don't believe in magic the way that children do, and that makes it very hard to bring it into their lives. But you, you do believe in me, and that way you help me make the magic real."

"Is it a secret? Should I not tell anyone?"

"Secrets are dangerous things," Till said, shaking her head. "Any grown up who tells a child to keep a secret is asking a bad thing. So I won't ask you not to tell anyone. But I have to warn you, when you do tell, like you said, they won't believe you."

"I *do* believe in you," Emma replied, sounding much older than she was. "I knew you were magic the first time you came to see me. I just knew it."

Gus heard the announcement that visiting hours were over, and sensed that Till was much too deep inside her own head at the moment to hear it. He moved past the open door and cleared his throat loudly.

Till looked up at him, and he lifted his gaze toward the clock. She nodded.

"Is he someone you know?" Emma asked, and Till couldn't help but laugh.

"He's a friend of mine."

"He's really cute."

Gus reddened, as did Till.

"Yes, he is," Till said softly. "I wish I didn't have to go, Emma, but I do. I won't see you again until after your operation. You have to be very brave for me, okay? Know that I'm never far away if you really need me."

If I only had a... Emma thought, wishing she had something to hold on to that would comfort her. The thought zipped across Till's mind and Till smiled sweetly.

"Watch this," she whispered, and she closed her eyes. A moment later there was a bump visible beneath the blanket covering Emma, and when Emma looked beneath, she gasped.

"A bear! Just the kind of bear that I was thinking of!"

"Just like that," Till smiled, blowing Emma a kiss through her mask. "Magic."

"He needs a name," Emma decided. "But I'm not real good at naming things."

Till analyzed the little bear for a moment, observing his features. "He looks like he needs a dignified name, like Remington. What do you think?"

"I think he's going to be my best friend," Emma said, hugging the bear close. "After you, Till. Will you be my best friend?"

"I'm a special kind of friend, Emma," Till replied, as she reluctantly moved toward the door. "And I'll always be nearby."

"Thank you," Emma whispered, putting a finger to her lips conspiratorially. *"Fairy Godmother."*

* * *

Till was silent on the ride home, and Gus couldn't stop himself from reaching across the seat and giving her hand a quick squeeze.

The moment he did so, the thoughts that had been rushing through her mind and into his stopped cold. It was an increasingly painful sensation for him, like running face first into a brick wall, every time her thoughts suddenly slammed shut on him. He couldn't help but wonder what it was she was thinking that she felt she had to hide from him so completely. He could only hope they weren't feelings that could do her harm.

"She believed you," he said softly. "Don't worry about that. And don't worry about her parents. I have a feelin' when she tells them where she got the bear, she'll tell them it came from the nice volunteer lady at the hospital. Ye may have told her she didn't have to keep a secret, but the child is wise. I don't think she'll be in a hurry to start tellin' people about her Fairy Godmother."

"She's so innocent, so trusting," Till whispered. "I worry for her, in a world like this one."

"That's what we're here for. To look out for the innocents, as best we can."

"I hope she's going to be okay tomorrow."

"She will be," Gus said, nodding once. "She has to be."

Till considered a moment and Gus felt the same certainty wash over her. "You're right, she will be. I don't know how I know, I just know."

"Ye've only sensed before when somethin' bad was gonna happen, Tilda Mae. Now is the time ye get to feel somethin' other than dread, for once."

"For once," Till sighed. "Not nearly often enough."

* * *

As morning broke, rain pounded down upon the roof, ran from the gutters in rivers, and steeped the already saturated lawn and flowerbeds.

If last winter had been one of the snowiest on record, Gus thought, this spring had to be one of the rainiest.

Till sat on the front porch, rocking on the swing. She was shielded from the showers, but not from the errant drops that blew past on the restless wind.

Her hair gathered glistening diamonds of water as it hung down against her soft, fair cheek. As he stood just a few feet away, Gus had to fight every urge inside of him; especially the one that howled for him to pick her up off that swing, carry her out into the rain, and kiss her there until they were both soaking wet.

He feared the thought may have transferred into her head before he could stop it, because she shivered where she sat and closed her eyes, seeming to be a million miles away from her current location.

Just as quickly as her eyes had closed they snapped open again. She was definitely aware of his presence, if not his specific, and explicit, desires.

"You going to just stand there, or are you going to join me?" she asked.

Gus shifted uneasily and ran a hand back through his hair. "Not sure. What do ye think, Tilda Mae?"

"Just sit with me a while," she said, dragging her feet against the porch to stop the swing. "You don't have to say anything."

Slowly he approached, and sat. He was quick to push the swing back into motion, and grasped the armrest with one hand to remind himself that he had better keep both as far away from her as possible. Still, he couldn't stop himself from asking a rather loaded question.

"If we were to talk today, what would we talk about?"

She sighed in response. Her thoughts, which had been jumbled and difficult to sort, now evaporated from his consciousness like sand swept away by rising tide.

"When do you get used to it, Gus?"

"To what?"

"To the... frustration in it all. To not being able to fix everything, and everyone."

"Not everyone struggles so with bein' unable to fix everythin' and everyone," he said, thinking how her idealistic temperament surely left her wide open for the hardest parts of being a Fairy Godmother, emotionally. "No one as much as ye do, I think."

"So." She turned to him, brushing a strand of damp hair out of her eyes. "What do I do with it?"

"Ye could try confidin' in me, as ye used to," he offered, but he knew that she wouldn't tell him what was really bothering her. If she was going to, she would have by now; and the layers of defense she'd built up around herself were so complete, so high, and so thick that he knew better than to try to breach them. To do so could be not only her undoing, but his as well.

Instinct told him to be patient; to watch and wait, and offer to be there. It was all that he could do.

"Maybe one day," she said wistfully, lifting her hand and bringing it toward his as if to hold it. She stopped at the last minute and dropped it back into her lap. "Maybe someday I will be able to tell you everything."

"Ye think?"

She smiled sadly. "I hope."

·

Chapter Twelve

The Last Loss

WITH ANOTHER DAY AT THE BOOKSTORE FINISHED, Gus and Till made their way home.

Before Gus had even parked the truck in the driveway he and Till exchanged a worried glance. There was something not right here. The energy surrounding the house, which was usually so welcoming, was overwhelmingly dark; poisoned by a sense of deep despair.

"What in the world…" Gus whispered, as he pulled the keys from the ignition. "Somethin's wrong with…"

"Lane," Till completed his sentence for him. "Something is very wrong with Lane."

"I'd better go have a word." He opened his door and prepared to walk around the front to open Till's, but she didn't wait for him this time. She had already hopped down from the cab and stood there, looking at him expectantly.

"Do you think I'm going to let you go alone into whatever this is that he's radiating? Not a chance."

The pair made their way up the Renter's Stairs and stood outside Lane's door. Usually, he would meet them at the threshold, so in tune to all around him that he knew when visitors were on their way. Tonight they heard a disturbing sound coming from beyond that door; one that matched the aura of sorrow projected from Lane's very soul.

He wasn't just weeping, he was sobbing.

Till knocked softly on the door. "Lane, do you want to talk?"

"Go away."

Till looked at Gus and bit her lip. Gus shook his head and sighed.

"C'mon then, man, isn't there anythin' we can do?"

"You can *go away!*" Lane shouted, his exclamation followed by the sound of shattering glass.

Gus watched as Till closed her eyes; she was gently turning her thoughts toward Lane. "I know you're hurt, Lane, I know that..." she whispered, reaching out in an attempt to offer what comfort she could as she seemed to make a startling discovery. "Oh, Lane."

"What is it? I couldn't read it," Gus replied, bewildered. He tried a second time and finally Lane allowed the thought to be known by him. "God, Lane, I'm sorry. Won't ye let us in?"

Lane unlatched the door from where he sat, then slumped down in a chair at the kitchen table with his head in his hands.

In all the time he'd lived in the house, Gus had never been in Lane's apartment before. He was surprised by what it contained. Lane apparently liked art: paintings adorned every wall. Mountains of books were piled in stacks on either side of the couch, but not really organized. The walls were painted scarlet, the ceiling dark blue. The effect gave the room the feeling of being caught in the glow of a continual sunset. It was as different from Gus's place as the two men were different from each other.

Till moved toward Lane, while Gus knew he dare not and lingered by the door.

"I'm so sorry," she said, "Is there anything at all I can do for you?"

"There's nothing anyone can do," Lane replied, looking up at her with bloodshot eyes and tear-stained cheeks. "Charlie is dead. He was my last charge, Till." It was as though by speaking the words aloud, Lane was trying to convince himself that they were true. "My last one; ninety-two years old. I knew him since the day... the day he was..." He dropped his head down again, his shoulders shaking as he continued to weep.

"I know it won't ever be the same, Lane, not without y'er longest-standin' charge to look after," Gus said now, moving forward slowly. "Surely, though, they'll assign ye someone soon."

"It wouldn't be the same, you know that," Lane growled. "Besides, they aren't going to be assigning me any new charges."

"What?" Till asked, surprised. "Why not?"

"I've been deemed too old to take on a new charge now. All my years of experience, all of the things I know and have seen, all going to waste because they want the next generation to do the job," he lamented.

When he looked up, Gus was struck again at how young Lane really looked. Fairy Godparents did not age at the rate of humanity, but still, for being more than two hundred years old, Lane looked as though he was still in his early thirties.

"Surely the university has other plans for ye, then. Ye've done so much work with the board…"

"Ah, yes, the grand council. I've done everything they asked me to and then some. But do they make me a full member? No. Why not? I have no idea. They are nothing now but a bunch of weak, feeble-minded fools." He drew a halting breath before continuing. "I'm a Fairy Godfather without charges, with only the task of babysitting the likes of YOU TWO left to live for? To watch the march of progress happen around me and know the parade is going to mow me down on the way through? Tell me, Leprechaun, does that sound like the kind of future *you'd* want?"

Gus said nothing, and Lane nodded. "I thought not. Who would? But that is my fate and I've got to suffer it. Still…" His voice dropped as he raised his eyes and wiped at them with the back of his hand. Till tried to move closer and squeeze his shoulders reassuringly, but he shook her hands away. He looked at both of them with the eyes of a stranger. "I am going to make my mark on the future of Fairy Godparents, I swear it. I know what has to happen, and if they think there's anyone better for that task than me, then they have *another thing coming.*"

"You need to rest, Lane. Why don't you lie down for a while?" Till encouraged, trying to draw his chair away from the table. She noticed only then that he had a silver flask clasped in his hand.

He's getting drunk? She thought to Gus.

Getting? I think he's already there, Gus thought back.

"I'll get drunk if I like, and you two young punks have nothing to say about it." Lane snarled, taking a slug from the flask. "Get out."

"Lane, let me bring you something to eat at least," Till begged.

"Get. Out." Lane motioned with his free hand and the door was thrown open all the way, back against the wall. "Go!"

Gus tried to gently lead Till away, but it took a moment before she was willing to allow it. He felt nothing but venom emanating from Lane now; not only directed toward life itself, but directed specifically toward him and Till, too. She may be too distraught or just too inexperienced to pick up on it, but there was only one word for the emotion that Lane was feeling when he looked at the pair of them. *Hatred.*

It worried Gus more than he wanted Till to know, and so he turned his thoughts toward calming her down and trying to reassure her, though he didn't know exactly how he was supposed to accomplish either goal.

"Don't tell me he'll be all right," Till cautioned, as the door slammed shut after them. "I won't believe you."

* * *

A few days later, Gus found himself parking his Chevy in a large, empty parking lot.

He glanced over at Till, who looked like a porcelain doll; her pale skin in stark contrast to her conservative, black dress. "Are ye ready?"

"As I will ever be."

The church was enormous, and imposing, and Gus felt a chill go through him as they walked through its wide open doors. He adjusted his tie. As unaccustomed as he was to wearing one, he wanted it to be on straight. For this occasion, he had made sure that his suit was flawless and his boots polished to a gleaming shine.

There was a casket at the front before the altar, and beside it stood Lane, exchanging words with the presiding priest.

"There's no one else here..." Till gasped, as she watched Lane take a seat in the front pew. "He's all alone."

"He had told me before that Charlie outlived his entire family," Gus whispered back. "In the end, Lane was all he had."

A moment later the organist began to play and a single, haunting voice filled the space, sounding like that of an angel as it sang a majestic requiem.

Till bit her lip as tears sprang to her eyes, and she moved into position on the kneeler in the very back pew.

Gus lowered himself down beside her, surprised, frankly, that Lane had not acknowledged their presence. Maybe he was too grief stricken to sense it in this moment, or maybe he just didn't care. Gus hoped maybe it meant something to Lane that someone other than himself had come to pay respects to the man Charlie had been.

Till didn't raise her eyes, or her head, for the duration of the service. Mass was conducted, even though there was no one for the priest to offer communion.

After the final hymn was sung and the service ended, Lane approached the priest and extended his hand. It was only then that he turned his head and seemed to take note that he was not the solitary mourner here.

"Excuse me a moment," Lane's voice rose, and Gus could feel now that he was unhappy that the pair had chosen to attend.

He rushed up to them, his eyes burning with anger. He spoke only one word. "Leave."

"Lane, we didn't want you to have to face this, or… the burial, alone…" Till whispered, but Lane raised his hand to her.

"You two, of all people, have no business here. Just get out, before I throw you out myself."

"Alright, we're goin'," Gus put his arm around Till protectively, escorting her away. Once they were out front, Till shook her head and gently extricated herself from Gus's half-embrace.

"He really has lost it, hasn't he?"

"Aye," Gus said, worried about the ramifications of Lane losing his last grip on sanity. "He has, Tilda Mae. He has." He could only wonder what that would mean, for them all.

* * *

That afternoon was a quiet one at the shop. Gus was on his own for a bit, with Till out on an errand to the bank and her parents at lunch.

The store had been empty for half an hour, but he suspected that soon the afternoon mommy crowd would come in before heading off to pick up their children from school, eager to snap up the newest paperbacks in Romance to take with them to the café nearby.

He was having a hard time concentrating on his work, simple a task though it was. His mind wandered where it inevitably did, and with Till otherwise engaged, he allowed himself the dangerous pastime of focusing on those thoughts of her, for just a moment.

He wasn't expecting to lose himself so completely that his mind blurred one thought into another; moments he remembered from the past, and ones that, though they seemed so real to him, he was absolutely certain had never occurred.

His mind flashed to a place he didn't recognize: a blank, white space all around. It was somehow familiar and yet entirely unknown. It was nowhere: a space between existence and whatever lay beyond it... and in that space, Till was asleep before his eyes.

Asleep? How is that possible? Till can't sleep anymore.

Just as quickly as the flash of what Gus could only call 'imagination' began it disappeared, and he came back to reality with a dull pounding in his head as the grating voice of one of their regular customers broke his reverie.

"Oh! There you are, Gus! Do you have that new one in the Fighting Highland Rogues series in yet?" She wiggled her eyebrows and Gus felt his face start to burn. Oh, how his regular customers loved to torment him with the title of that particular book series...

"Aye, I believe it just came in. I was about to unpack them."

"Oh." Mrs. Hamilton bounced up and down on her sensible black pumps. "Do you think you could go and get one for me now? Train trip coming up this weekend, I just have to have it!"

"*I'd* be happy to get it for you," Till said, joining the conversation and coming, once again, to Gus's rescue. Upon seeing her, the woman's mood seemed to sour.

"Why thank you, Till. I'll just... wait by the cash register."

"Be right there." As the woman headed off, Till paused, looking at Gus sideways. "Are you all right? You look like you've just seen a ghost."

"Just a wee bit of a headache, Tilda Mae. I'll be fine." He started stocking the books once more, wishing he could convince himself that what he'd seen in his head was nothing more than the manifestation of his worst fear playing out in his subconscious mind and dragging his conscious thoughts along with it.

"If you say so." She shook her head. "I'll get you a cup of coffee while I'm back there. Might help."

"Thank ye kindly," Gus replied. The moment she'd gone, he closed his eyes and leaned back against the wall. The room seemed to spin whenever she came too near to him these days, and he didn't, for the life of him, have any idea how to stop its frenzied rotation.

What he'd envisioned had to be his worst fear; something serious being wrong with Till. What terrified him now was the nagging feeling that what he'd seen wasn't simply an odd sort of daydream, but a glimpse, somehow, into an inescapable future event. That waking nightmare felt more like a vision— and the vision felt like a warning.

He'd never had an episode of pure foresight before, but he had sure heard enough talk about them from his grandmother while she was alive to give him pause now. The potential that it was an ability he may develop somewhere along the line was something that he pushed to the very back of his thoughts; something that he didn't want to have to deal with, and so refused to even consider, unless and until it became impossible to escape considering it.

The day had come today, though, in which his heart told him that not only did he have to consider it, but he must regard it as a serious sign. Till's future was in jeopardy, from some danger as yet unknown.

Would he be able to help her — to save her, if need be — when that dreaded time came?

Till reappeared, carrying a steaming hot cup of coffee. "Here you go."

Gus's hands trembled as he reached out for it.

"Hey…" she said, taking immediate note and putting one of her hands on top of his to try to steady the tremor. "Are you sure you're all right?"

"Yeah."

"Why don't you take a few minutes in the back? I've got things covered out here."

"Thanks," he said, struggling not to spill the coffee as he attempted to free his hand from hers.

As soon as he was in the back, Gus set the cup down, untouched, and hurried into the office. He slumped down into the nearest chair and allowed his head to fall into his hands.

He forced his mind to picture Till at the front register, looking fine and acting normally, and he tried to convince himself again that what he'd seen meant nothing. Those more comforting thoughts were then intruded upon by the memories of her forgetting what she was, and where she was supposed to be going. Those moments fueled the flames of his panic.

As he closed his eyes, again he saw the image of her lying on the ground in a pure white space; only this time instead of trying to drive the sight from his mind, he tried to focus on it; to gather as much information as he could.

He startled as the hazy forms of three shadows appeared in the space as well; one standing across from Till, and the others standing beside her. He couldn't tell from the rough smudges that made out their outlines whether the others were male or female; if they were strangers or people he knew.

He only knew that in this place, Till was frightened, she was vulnerable, and she was in grave danger.

He felt dizzier than before and suddenly ill, and regretted the fact that he'd eaten anything today.

Chapter Thirteen

Turncoat

GUS ROSE SLOWLY AND DRESSED, preparing to face another day.

He analyzed his face in the mirror but not for more than a second; he didn't need it to confirm he looked as tired as he felt.

When did I start to feel so old? he wondered.

His mind turned then to another, much older Fairy Godfather. He attempted to direct his thoughts toward Lane, to reach out to him, but it was no use. The man was completely out of reach physically and emotionally, therefore, for the moment at least, he was beyond Gus's ability to help.

He and Till both had the day off, but he still turned up on her front porch about the normal time they'd have morning coffee together. He gazed up at the pale blue sky for a moment as he waited for her to appear. It was a halfway decent day weather-wise for once. But suddenly, it felt as if the temperature of the atmosphere dropped by at least twenty degrees — the moment Till opened the door.

She was seriously shaken, and Gus quickly surmised it was by something that had just happened. It worried him that he'd had no sense of her distress as he'd approached her physical location, but whatever the reason, at least she saw no need to shield her current distress from him now. That reassured him that there was a chance she might seek his help this time.

No matter what the situation, he always listened to her before saying anything. He'd learned that when it came to Till, her thoughts were only the tip of the proverbial iceberg; there was always much more beneath than he could readily pick up on. This time, though, he had to prod her to speak.

"Want to talk about it?"

"No," she replied flatly, and then shifted her weight. "Yes. No. I don't know."

"I can try piecin' it together myself," he offered.

She finally relented. "No. We should talk, but not here." She looked around nervously, as though certain that the walls had eyes, ears, and telepathic capabilities.

"Where do ye want to go?"

"Surprise me," she said, and she held out her hands to him.

"There's a place I like to go when I need to think," he began.

"Anywhere, I don't care," she interrupted. "As long as we're alone and *very* far from here."

Gus nodded. He took hold of her hands and closed his eyes, and an instant later they were standing at the edge of a sandy beach, surrounded by rolling hills.

She gasped softly, and Gus smiled. The isle did tend to have that effect on people, truly seeing it for the first time.

Sure, she'd briefly led him to Ireland during their hide and seek game, but she hadn't seen anything like Barleycove Beach.

Gus suddenly had mixed emotions about having her here. By showing her his refuge, he risked losing it; memories of her being here would change it for him forever. But he knew that she needed him to listen now, and in a place not so easily observable by those who would pry. He had a pretty good idea already who was most likely to make the attempt.

"It's Lane," she announced, confirming his suspicions as she bent down to untie her shoes. She abandoned them on the edge of the beach and then took her first tentative steps into the sand.

Gus kept his boots on and fell into stride beside her. "What's he done now?"

"He came to me this morning. Marched right into my thoughts without so much as asking permission." Her speech was pressured, and though she continuously looked around her, she was clearly too preoccupied to take in the full scope of the beach's beauty. "I told him to stop, to get out of my head and to speak to me aloud as if I was only human. That upset him. Finally, after he got the picture that I was not going to let him stay in my mind, let alone go poking around in it, he said what he had to say."

Gus's stomach sank. He had a feeling he knew what Lane had on his mind.

"He warned me, Gus, that he's watching us. He's keeping his eyes open for any indication that we may be 'taking liberties with the rules', as he put it. And that's not all..." She then thought something so unsettling, Gus's jaw clenched in response.

"Did he, then?" he said through gritted teeth. "He wants ye to spy on Hannah?"

"To put it bluntly, yes. He said that he knows she's just one more infraction away from being sent back to the university for retraining, or worse. He said they could take her powers away." Till stopped walking and looked up at Gus plaintively. "Surely she can't have done anything bad enough to warrant *that*."

"I don't know what Hannah has or hasn't done, but I do know this: I won't have him houndin' ye this way. I'm going to put a stop to it."

"Oh, no, Gus, please don't get involved," Till begged, tugging at his sleeve. "If you do, he'll only get worse. I keep hoping if we just keep doing our job, the way we're supposed to, in time he'll get tired of finding nothing to go after and just give up. Move on to something else."

"No one knows better than I that Lane is like a bulldog when he wants somethin'," Gus warned. "He will not, cannot let go of it. Y'er going to have to mind yer thoughts around him as best ye can. Keep him out of everythin', no matter how trivial it is. Make yer mind a no trespassin' zone. Do whatever you can to protect yerself from his interference." He looked at her sadly. "Tilda Mae, we may have to take much more drastic action than either of us has wanted to consider before now."

She knew what he meant; he meant going to the university's governing board. She recoiled at the thought.

"Even if they would grant us an audience, would you really want one? To go in there with all of them so close to your thoughts and..." she choked the last words out, "judging you."

"No," Gus relented. "Not at all."

"Neither would I," she concluded. "Why is Lane so hell bent on destroying all of our futures?" Till asked. "He lived in that house for years, before I got there. I thought we were family."

"Nothin' is as dangerous as an angry man with nothin' left to lose." Gus sighed. "That is exactly what Lane has become."

At last she admitted a truth that Gus had known for some time. "He actually frightens me."

"Don't be afraid," he said, leaning closer as they continued walking. "I'm always standin' just over yer shoulder."

"I worry for you too, where he is concerned, Gus. I—" Till stopped suddenly, shaking her head as if to force the thoughts and emotions she didn't want out of it.

"Here, now, none of that. I can look after myself. I just... I wish I could help ye more," Gus said softly, his eyes shifting out to the advancing and retreating tide.

"You help just by being who you are." Till looked up and drew in a deep breath. Suddenly her senses awoke to the beauty all around her, and she was clearly taken aback by it. She admired the view for a long moment before continuing.

"You never talk about your past here," she said. "I know some, you know that, just from roaming around in your head all the time I've known you. I know that you spent part of your life living near here..." Her eyes misted over as she lifted a hand to touch his arm but stopped short, allowing it to fall slowly back to her side. "You've walked many miles up and down this beach. Alone."

Gus knew there was no point in trying to conceal what this place meant to him; it would be impossible, even if he tried. "I came to live in Cork when I was fifteen," he began. His eyes took on a distant stare, and he watched Till's posture stiffen for a moment. She had, despite his best efforts, sensed the pain in his heart at the thought of times gone past.

"Ma's parents lived nearby. I came to live with them after..."

Till gently searched his thoughts and Gus allowed it: to a point.

"After your father died."

"Aye. But I didn't stay long. Day I turned seventeen, I set off to runnin' and I didn't look back. By then, my grandfather had joined my parents in the grave. I don't think he ever got over the loss of his little girl. Whatever else Ma was, she was always his little girl."

Till listened intently, slowing her pace to match his as memory dragged him backwards in time, and his feet fought the sand to keep moving forward.

"Grandmother was frail, and dyin', and I knew it," Gus continued, looking down at his boots as he spoke. "I couldn't take watchin', and she didn't want me to have to. So I was... not at her side the night she finally left this life."

Till reached over now and took hold of his arm. "Gus, you were just a kid. You did the best you could. You certainly can't hold yourself responsible, after all that you'd already lost, for the fact that you couldn't stand to be there one night out of all the nights you spent with her." Till correctly sensed that his grandmother had not died alone, and pressed further into his memory. "Her sister was with her, and you know that your grandmother loved you more than anything else in this world."

"That's why it's so difficult now," he whispered, stopping where he stood and gazing out to sea, then up at the billowing, downy heavens. "She loved me best in this world, and I let her down."

Suddenly Gus shivered, not only at the pain of his own memories but from the fact that the warmth he'd felt radiating from Till suddenly stopped; replaced by that cold, impenetrable barrier. He could not retreat any further into her head or heart for comfort, and it made him ache, all the more.

Till released his arm and took what appeared to be a determined step backward, putting at least two feet of space between their bodies. Gus wanted nothing more in this moment than to bridge that gap and pull her close to his heart.

God, Till, hold me, please... he thought, before he could stop himself.

When he gathered the courage to look up at her again, Till had lost what little color remained in her face; her eyes overflowed with tears, and she stayed planted firmly where she stood. She thought something to him before she could catch herself, and it meant almost as much to Gus as the physical comfort of her arms would have.

If only I could.

The thought lingered in the air between them as the sky turned dark and the sea roared up, crashing into the sand.

"Change in the weather," Till whispered. "We had better get back."

Gus nodded. His heart broke all over again, and he closed his eyes a moment, taking refuge behind his own mental battlements. They could be unforgiving, too, and impregnable as stone, keeping her from reading his thoughts now just as she was doing with him.

How was it possible they kept growing closer in so many ways, even while he was forced to wage an internal war to keep them apart?

How could he continue to keep from her how desperately he loved her, how deeply every part of him longed for her, how he knew that nothing in the universe meant more to him than she did, even though by rights and by rules, it should?

His resolve was weak this night, and he found himself especially grateful that she seemed bound and determined to keep physical and mental distance between them.

Tonight, if left up to him, he knew that the walls would crumble, and the two of them would be buried together beneath the ruins.

* * *

Gus was exhausted, emotionally and physically, by the time they transported back to the house. Till had done most of the work of getting them there, sensing his vulnerability in the moment. She was far too kind to do so in an obvious manner; she simply and silently supplemented his powers with her own in order to return them to where they needed to be.

He stood with her on the front porch and watched as she gestured slightly. The door unlocked and opened just a little, allowing a shaft of light from the inside to pierce the darkness.

She stood still for only a second before him, half in light and half in shadow. In that instant, something so primal, so deep within him stirred that his soul cried out to hers; and Till trembled as she realized that he was struggling beneath the weight of a burden that was too great for him to carry on his own.

He knew she could not speak of it, any more than she could speak of whatever it was that troubled her so these days. Yet Gus felt certain that whatever battles they were fighting, they would continue to try to help each other cope as best they could. Tonight, he just wasn't himself; and he thought a silent apology to her for needing to hurry on his way.

I'm drownin', Tilda Mae. Sometimes, I really feel like I'm drownin'.

I know, she thought to him. *I know, and I'm so sorry, Gus. I wish there was more I could do to help you.*

Despite the fact that every last rational thought told him he should run, he followed her as she walked into the house; uncertain why, and uncertain why she did not try to stop him.

She walked into her bedroom and he hovered in the doorway a moment, terrified to follow.

She stood motionless before the large cheval mirror he'd created for her, to adorn the room out of her very daydreams. She appeared to be something divine... light filtering through sheer curtains caressing her delicate face— so beautiful he found it difficult to catch his breath. She looked like he imagined the mythical pride of Pygmalian: a work of art as pure and every bit as flawless. Also, he feared, just as fragile.

He moved toward her as she remained frozen in front of the mirror, staring so deeply into it, it was as though she didn't even see her own reflection. Her head tilted slightly to the side when at last he whispered her name.

Before he knew what he was doing, Gus placed his arms around her waist, clasping his hands against her stomach and resting his chin on her shoulder. Her hair smelled like roses, as it always did, and he closed his eyes. Gently and without any music he began to sway slowly from side to side and her hips, at first resistant and unaffected, began to move with him. Till's breath left her body in one long exhalation, and she fell back against him as if leaning into him, closer to him, almost becoming a part of him, was the most natural thing in the world.

He almost forgot himself in that moment for one reason alone: that reason being he desperately wanted to forget himself. What was more, he wanted her to forget herself, too, and for them both to become lost to the same passion that had consumed them the night his One Wish was granted by her with such a deep and tender reverence.

God, how I want you, Tilda Mae, he thought, and he parted his lips to speak into her ear once more when the reality of where he was and what he was about to do returned to his consciousness.

This was no dream, and she was no fantasy. She was real, flesh and blood in his arms, and wanted her more than he had ever wanted anything in his life.

But to have her would be mean losing her, and he couldn't allow it. Not now, not when she was so vulnerable, especially. It was his job to try to get to the bottom of what was happening to her, not to make things worse by satisfying his own needs and desires, even if they seemed in this moment so entirely matched to hers.

Till finally spun herself around in his arms and leaned in, eyes closed, to kiss his mouth.

"Tilda Mae," he groaned, in agony beyond anything he'd ever felt before, as he forced himself to step back from her. "We can't."

"But why not? Gus, what did I do wrong?"

"You didn't do anything wrong, Till, it's just... don't you remember? I can't... we just can't."

"Remember? Remember what?"

Gus brought his hands to his lips, clasping them to keep a shout of frustration and horror from coming to fruition. Her memory was obviously lapsing again, and he was beside himself. He shook his head in denial; all he could do, damn him, was shake his head and back away.

Till crumpled to the bed and stayed there, and Gus knew he had no choice but to leave her where she was. If he touched her once more, again, now, anywhere at all, there would be no turning back. This night would become another like the only night they were ever meant to have, and who knew what that would possibly do to make the memory loss she was already suffering worse.

"I'm sorry," he whispered, kneeling down beside her but daring not reach out. "So sorry, Tilda Mae. Forgive me." Then he did the only thing he could do for the moment: he left her alone, feeling as if his stricken heart was being crushed between her ashen fingers.

* * *

Soon after, Gus lay on his own bed, staring at a ceiling that never changed, though somehow he always expected it to.

He felt lost, and defeated.

His mind was fixed upon the moment that had passed between them there, standing upon the shores of home, when every part of him fought the fact that he didn't know if he could bear his burdens alone any longer. Till had responded with an understanding beyond his comprehension. Her reaction to his heartache only made him love her more. Then they'd come back, and she'd reached for him as if it was something she was completely accustomed to. Her heart broke, as his did, when he'd been forced to pull away.

He knew that he would be able to think of nothing, and no one else tonight, save the woman who had given him everything to grant his One Wish, and the tender, passionate way in which she'd done it.

Chapter Fourteen
Consequences

GUS WAS SWEEPING UP THE FRONT WALK, using the broom instead of magic, as was his custom. It was something he did when he wanted to think, puttering around the yard, and found that Till was right; doing things the old fashioned way still soothed the mind better than magic ever could.

The sun was beginning to rise, and it was usually about this time that Hannah would come stomping out of the house, in shoes totally impractical for her job as a waitress. He knew that they helped with her tips, though, so she was willing to suffer the pain of wearing them to get maximum benefit from her human-world employment.

He did not expect to see, instead, Hannah pulling up in a very small, very expensive looking sports car.

She was on the passenger side and she opened the door for herself, indicating immediately that the man driving— and Gus was sure it was a man—was no gentleman.

He heard her giggle through the open window and looked away. He set the broom aside and prepared to go into the house. Whatever was about to happen, if anything, he didn't want to know.

"That's it!" A triumphant, familiar sounding voice crowed. Gus looked up to see Lane peering into the car, where Hannah was still trying to extricate herself from the kiss the driver was now planting on her.

"Lane!" she cried, getting out and trying to smooth down her tousled hair. "I can explain."

"Explain it to the board," Lane said, as he tugged her back toward the house by her arm and the driver sped away.

Gus rushed forward. Lane had no right to man-handle Hannah that way, no matter what she may have done. He reached the pair in a few swift strides. "Hands off!"

"Gus, don't let him take me before the board!" Hannah pleaded. "Don't let him take me anywhere!"

Gus pried Hannah's arm from Lane's grasp. "Step back, man, I'm warnin' ye. That's no way to treat a lady."

"She's no lady," Lane retorted, turning red. "And she will answer to the governors for what she's done."

"Gus!" Hannah cowered behind him, in tears.

"Go into the house, Hannah, right now." Gus sent Hannah forward with a gentle push and put himself between her and Lane. "I said step off."

Lane's responded with a haughty laugh. "It's too late. She's already gone."

Gus looked over and saw it was true, Hannah had vanished. He grabbed hold of Lane by the shirt and pulled him up off his feet, leaving him dangling above the ground. "What did you *do to her*?"

"Hannah has abused her powers too often, and now she's going to pay for it."

"How?"

"Not for me to decide," Lane said, wresting himself free from Gus's grip and dropping back to earth. "But believe me, I wish it were."

"I believe it," another voice spoke up. Till appeared, still wearing her bathrobe. "What have you done, Lane?"

"Why does everyone think this is *my* fault?" Lane snapped. "I'm just doing what I have already done for almost two centuries; *my job*. Before your great-great-grandparents walked this earth, I have been doing my job. So maybe I know a little bit more about it than you think, and maybe you two should mind your own business."

"Will we be able to speak to someone on Hannah's behalf?" Gus asked.

Lane shook his head. "You couldn't get an audience with the board of governors if you were the last Fairy Godparent alive, Leprechaun. They keep their own counsel. I'm sure they wouldn't have anything to learn from the likes of you. As for Hannah, she has a lot to learn from people like *me*."

Till's voice trembled with rage. "Get out."

Now Lane's laugh was short and indignant. "What?"

"I said GET OUT!" Till screamed. "Get the hell out of my house and stay out! You're not welcome here anymore."

"You're not serious, Tilda Mae..." Lane sputtered. "Your Aunt—"

"Isn't here." Gus said, backing up so he was now standing between Lane and Till. "The lady said to pack yer things, Lane. I suggest ye do as she says."

"When I get home tonight, I expect you to be gone, Lane." Till repeated. "For good."

"If that's really the way you feel about it," Lane said, turning back toward the house. "Then I won't have to even set foot in the place again to take it all. You have no clue, little girl, do you? You have no idea just how powerful I am."

With a grand wave of his hand, a bright light emanated from the windows of his apartment, and then a moment later, he was gone.

Till took off at a run, back toward the house with Gus on her heels.

She bolted to the Renter's Stairs and when she burst through the door of Lane's apartment, she found it completely empty; even the walls and ceiling had paled from their deepest hues to blinding white. "My God..." she whispered, "It's like he was never here."

"We should have been so lucky..." Gus replied. His next words conveyed a grave warning. "This is nowhere near over."

Till shivered and folded her arms over her chest. "What will they do to Hannah?"

Gus sighed and ran his hand over the scruff on his chin. "Not sure. The only person I ever knew who was retrained for abuse of power was a guy everyone talked about my first year at DCTU. Poor soul, he was held up to us all as a bad example. He was confined to a small dormitory buildin' somewhere on campus until he completed retrainin'. I never did hear what became of him after that."

"Can we help her?"

"I don't know, Till. I just don't know."

Till rushed forward, and all at once she was in his arms. He was shocked, and as he tried to shield his thoughts from her, he found that he reacted by automatically dropping his arms to his sides and taking a huge step back.

The look of pain on her face was unlike anything he'd ever seen—she was so hurt by his response that she turned and rushed from the room.

"Till!" he called after her, but it was no use.

He'd have to give her a little time to get over the sting of what she perceived as rejection, and he needed all the time he could get, knowing he'd never get over, or used to, the fact that he'd been forced to push her away.

Chapter Fifteen
Around The Block Once More

GUS WORRIED WHAT SORT OF STATE Till would be in as he waited for her to answer the door that evening.

He found she appeared quickly and seemed preoccupied, but not as distressed as when he'd last left her.

He knew that she'd been pacing. It was an activity she didn't often undertake, but when she did he knew because the old floors creaked, and the sound of her footfalls resonated up through the air returns in the house and into his apartment.

"Is there anything ye'd like to talk about?" He looked down at the floor then back up at her. "About what happened with Lane, maybe?" He knew her mind must still be on Lane, though he couldn't get much of a read on her.

"I don't know if it'd help, but I feel like I'm going to jump out of my skin," she admitted. "I don't know what to do with myself."

"Feel like takin' a walk?"

"Don't have all that much time before we have to go to work. I want to check in on Violet tonight. See how that new babysitter we arranged is working out."

Gus was relieved that for now, her memory seemed to be working correctly again and she knew that they had Godparenting duties to attend to later on. He held back a sigh of relief. "We don't have to go far. Just a lap around the block and back."

Till nodded and grabbed her raincoat. "Let's go."

They walked on in silence for a little while, until it was nearly time to turn the corner from Finch Street onto Dell. At last Till drew a deep breath and spoke. "I can't believe I threw him out, Gus. I just can't believe it."

"Ye had no choice, Till. He left ye no other option."

"Are you sure?" She glanced at him sideways. "I keep wondering what Aunt Tilda would say if she could talk to me now."

"She'd say that ye did what ye had to do to protect the rest of our fairy family. Even if that meant one of them had to go." He paused, hating to say what he was about to say next, but feeling as though it may bring her some comfort. "Besides, the Lane that ye asked to leave is not the same Lane that Aunt Tilda knew and cared about. He's a stranger to us now; and I am certain, were she still with us, dear soul, he would be to her, too." He let his words sink in before adding, "Ye can always invite him back later on, if things change. It's not like the house will sink without his rent."

"True." Till pulled her collar up tighter around her throat. "For now… what do I… what do *we* do, Gus?"

Gus's heart skipped at the sound of the word 'we'.

'We' implied there was something more to just the two of them than individuals. 'We' implied there was, somehow, an *'us'*.

He blinked and tried to keep his mind focused on giving an answer. "Lane's chosen his path. We have to stay on our guard, and make sure it intersects ours as infrequently as possible."

Gus shoved his hands into the pockets of his jacket as he walked. The sun was just beginning to sink, and as soon as that light dimmed, the temperature rapidly dropped.

He wished that he could hold Till's hand to help keep it warm, he saw her cupping them together and blowing on them and realized she must have forgotten her gloves again. He decided that if he couldn't do the former, at least he could do something about the latter.

An instant later, Till stared at her hands in surprise; she was wearing her gloves. She still never thought of using her powers in terms of bringing things to her that she may have forgotten.

"Thank you," she said, and he watched with satisfaction as her entire body seemed to relax at the sensation of warming against the chill.

He took Till in again as she walked, her face half in light of the waning day and half in darkness from the trees above. He marveled.

This willowy, slight being, with her still-more-human-than-fairy ways, had entranced him from the moment he first saw her. Time only served to deepen and intensify his amazement, and he wondered how deeply he would feel it in one… five… ten years' time.

He wondered how deeply it was possible to feel, at all; certain that whatever he believed the limits were, that Till could take him beyond them, if only allowed to try.

He had to fight his thoughts now, as she walked along the road at his side, seeming quite immersed, still, in her own.

His memories of the night she'd granted his One Wish seemed to become more vivid by the day. They almost felt tangible at times; something you could reach out and touch if your arms were just a little longer. Forever exceeding his grasp but always within his line of vision, even when he tried his best to banish the images, emotions, sensations, and experiences from his mind. They never truly relented, just retreated into the periphery. Her tenderness beckoned him like a lonely siren; only to retreat at the last minute and fade away, as if she knew somehow that to truly possess him would bring about his ruin.

He watched her skirt sway at her knees, diverting wandering eyes from the hips that moved slightly from side to side as she walked. He knew every curve of her body, so well he could remember each in exact detail. Every freckle, tiny scar, every gentle slope and enticing softness, forever new and fresh in his memory.

He didn't know how he could stand it sometimes— wanting her so much, and knowing that he would never be able to have her that way again. It seemed the most natural, and was the most instinctual thing in the world to him to want to be physically tender with her. To bring her comfort with his touch in ways that nothing else could, in times of heartache as well as happiness.

He'd ached with longing at seeing her smile before. Seeing her cry nearly brought him to his knees, and seeing her frightened made him want to turn his desire toward her in all of its roaring intensity. To protect her, to console her, by making love to her so gently she would forget anything had ever frightened her, and everyone else in the world while he held her so.

"Did you hear me?" she asked, stopping and waving at him.

"Sorry... I was lost somewhere for a moment there. Say it again, please?"

"I said, I can't help but wonder if Aunt Tilda's death has something to do with the change in Lane. It's difficult for me to know, because I met him just days before she left us. I wondered what you think about that?"

"Makes sense," Gus replied. "Lane was always an extreme person, as long and as well as I've known him. But y'er right, he got much worse about the time Tilda took to weakenin'. She was still pretty spry when I moved in, it was really only in the last two years that she started to show her age, and the signs that things were comin' to an end for her."

"It was hard for me to see, and I knew her such a short time before…" Till said softly, leaving the thought unfinished. "It must have been terrible for the rest of you."

"I don't know if anythin' is more difficult than watchin' someone ye care about decline. To see them become so fragile." He shivered at the memory of the first time he'd heard a crash and hurried to Aunt Tilda's side to find she'd fallen. Even her magic had not been enough to save her from the frailties that eventually overtake all living things… even those who live to be three hundred years of age before it happens. "If it was hard for any of us to see, it had to be most difficult for Lane. He had known her so many years, so much longer than the rest of us."

"Any idea how long?" Till asked. "He never would tell me and I never could get a read on that."

Gus rolled his eyes up towards the sky as he thought. "Had to be at least two hundred years. From the stories she told me alone of when he was first introduced to the fairy world, must have been."

"Two *hundred* years…" She shook her head. "I can't begin to imagine how well you'd know someone if you'd been friends with them for two hundred years."

I can… Gus thought, and then again, tried to stamp out the power of the thought before she picked up on it.

"I believe that they were a lot closer than Lane will admit to anyone," Till continued. "Maybe something in him just snapped when he lost his closest companion." Her tone changed, and her voice failed with the next words she attempted to speak. She tried but couldn't quite get them out, no matter what she did.

"It's all right," Gus said softly. He didn't need to be able to read her mind or hear her say the words to know what she was thinking; the fearful, melancholy look in her eyes said it for her. "I can't imagine bein' without ye either, Till."

Silence settled between them again, and they realized that they had walked back around and down Finch Street and passed up the house.

Till stopped and looked longingly at the stretch of road ahead of them, as though she wished the moment didn't have to end and they could stall off their return to the real world for just a little bit longer.

"We have time for once more around the block, I think," Gus answered. "If ye'd like."

She nodded gently, and for an instant it looked like she wanted to reach out and loop her arm through his. Gus caught the faintest whisper of sound emanating from her mind, though he only had a moment to translate it before it was snatched away from him again.

It was music. She was thinking of a song; just the melody, though that alone spoke volumes to him, and nothing more was needed for him to understand. The song in her head and heart right now was the same one they'd danced to in the bookshop.

Y'er the only dance partner in the world for me, Tilda Mae, and ye always will be.

A look crossed her face that told him that he may not have hid that thought as well as he'd hoped.

All he could do was shove his hands deeper into his jacket pockets, stare at the gravel beneath his boots, and walk on.

Chapter Sixteen

Moving On

GUS WATCHED PEOPLE WALK PAST as an enormous plane sat on the tarmac just beyond security. Still, majestic, and a sight to behold, even for someone with powers beyond the norm.

Ryan's mother, Nancy, rifled through her purse and pulled out their tickets. She looked up at the board announcing departure times and nodded with satisfaction.

"Now boarding," she said softly, before extending her hand toward Gus. "New life starts now."

"I hope and pray it's a much brighter one," Gus said, shaking her hand. She grasped hold and pulled him into a hug, and Gus politely patted her on the back before letting go. "Now remember, ye promised to write."

"The café has wireless, I'll be able to email and so will Ryan. I promise we'll keep you updated."

"And you promised you'd come visit," Ryan said softly. "Don't forget that."

"Ye should know by now, Ryan, I am nothin' if not a man of my word."

"Truer words were never spoken." Suddenly he grasped hold of Gus's shoulders and pulled him into a fierce hug. "Thank you, Gus. For everything. I promise, I'm going to make you proud. And I want you to be there when I graduate."

The lump in Gus's throat kept him from speaking now; all he could do was nod.

"Now boarding flight 2140 nonstop service to Tampa," a voice declared, and Gus nodded toward the security checkpoint.

"Ye'd better hurry, don't want to miss yer flight." He picked up Ryan's small suitcase and handed it to him. "Remember, no one else can make y'er future. It's in yer hands now."

"I'll remember."

Gus stood back and observed as the two cleared security and rushed forward toward the gate on the other side.

"Thank you," the young man mouthed back to Gus once more. Gus raised a hand, giving a single wave.

He waited until the plane taxied out of sight before slowly making his way back to his truck.

* * *

Gus ambled from his truck up the driveway. He'd taken the spot furthest from the house, hoping that if he parked behind the other cars and went in quietly that no one would know that he was back.

Saying goodbye, even temporarily, to Ryan was harder than he thought it'd be. He had so many worries for the lad, even if he was going to be living in a much safer environment from now on. He wondered how Ryan would adjust to a new mentor, but knew he would just have to have faith that his Fairy Godfather brethren would look after the boy and his mother with the same care that Gus had.

It was the first time Gus had ever been severed from a charge, and even if for the good of that charge, the experience stung.

As he approached the house, a projected thought entered his mind before he saw the person who had sent it.

Good evening.

Is it? he thought back, approaching Till where she sat on the front porch swing.

"I think so," she said, gesturing for him to join her if he wished. "Ryan is on his way to a better world; I think that makes it a very good evening." She stopped the motion of the swing long enough to allow Gus to take a seat beside her. They stayed still upon it, in suspension, as he exhaled slowly.

He ran a hand back through his shaggy dark hair. "Ye are right, I know ye are. It's just…"

Hard to say goodbye? she thought, knowing that the words would be too difficult for him to hear aloud.

"Yeah."

"You know you'll still get to see him now and then," she tried to reassure him, but it became clear he was not going to be so easily consoled tonight. She backpedaled. "Sorry. I have no right to try to tell you how to handle any of this, you know so much more about the whole Fairy Godparenting thing than I do."

"Don't think I know more about feelin' alone," he said, the thought turning to words before he could stop it.

Till looked down, her hair obscuring her features. "I do know a little about that." Another thought occurred to her and she looked up at him again. "Were you able to find anything out about Hannah?"

"She's definitely being kept on the campus. But that's all I could find out, for the time bein'. It's difficult to gather much information. I'm hopin' that I'll be able to pick somethin' up if I keep one ear to the ground."

He read her next thought and nodded. "I promise, ye'll be the first to know."

"Thank you."

He sensed her mood shift, and hoped a change of subject would bring her at least a few moments' peace. "It's a beautiful night. The house, the garden, it all looks grand."

"Of course, everything looks better at night," Till opined. "It's dark. You can't see the flaws."

"Flaws?"

"House needs a new coat of paint, the garden needs to be weeded. Can't see that at night, so everything looks better."

"I disagree," Gus answered, pulling back and then pushing his feet off the ground, propelling the swing into motion. "Things aren't hidden at night. They're distilled down to their purest form. Shadow and substance play against each other, and in starlight ye see things the way that they really are."

Till glanced at him sideways, her eyes large and sad. Her thoughts of current time and place melted away before him, and her mind again appeared to him as a slate with nothing on it.

"Why do ye *do that*?" he whispered, unable to hold back the question any longer. The hurt he felt at her blatant retreat bled through in his voice. "Why do ye hide from me now, Tilda Mae?" He redirected his eyes and focused on the ground as it rushed past. "So often, and after all this time. It... never used to be so."

Till bit her lip and shook her head. She closed her eyes, appearing to be in great distress. A single thought escaped her ability to shield it, and it echoed in Gus's head.

Some things are better left alone.

"Some things, or some people?"

"Both."

"Aye..." He stomped his boots down and stopped the swing. "That they are." He rose and turned to go.

"Gus, wait."

He looked back at her, questioning.

"Has the idea ever occurred to you that maybe there is a good reason why you can't always read me anymore? That maybe there's something there that would be to your detriment to know?"

"Have a hard time believin' that it's anythin' I couldn't handle." His defenses kicked in full force and he tried to shield her, as well, from just how deeply hurt he felt that she would continually hold back.

"Please," she whispered, rising slowly upon knees that were visibly shaking. "Don't ask me. It's hard enough not to be able to..." She held her arms open in a hopeless gesture.

"Not to be able to what?"

Her head hung low. "Tell you everything anymore."

Gus's chest hurt, and he knew he'd better step back. Whatever it was she was keeping from him, she was doing it for a reason, and at great emotional cost. For tonight, at least, he felt he had better respect that.

His shoulders slumped in defeat. "Hard to know, too. Goodnight, Tilda Mae."

"Please don't be angry with me," she pleaded, and the fact she felt the need to ask hurt him all the more.

"I'm not angry, Till, promise. Just... sorry."

"Me too." Her voice now quaked as her knees did. "You have no idea how sorry."

* * *

Gus wandered up to his apartment, still staring down at his boots. A chapter in his life was ending, no matter how he looked at it. Ryan would be moving on to a new Fairy Godfather, and he would, sooner or later, be matched to another charge.

Aside from Maggie, Ryan had been Gus's only charge for a while, and he kept wondering when they were going to increase his workload. He'd been told that he had workload enough keeping his eye on Till and her charges as well, but he wondered if he was doing enough.

He always wondered, especially where Till was concerned, if he was doing enough. The other side of that particularly expensive coin was wondering if he was doing too much— and it was a question he had yet to find a satisfactory answer to.

Perhaps that's the trouble with life, Gus thought. *There really exists no such thing as a happy medium. Medium is miserable at worst, or at best still leaves you staring out windows and up into the sky wondering what, exactly, could have been instead.*

He stood a long while in the hot shower, noting that no matter how many times he sought comfort there from the chill in his heart, it never went away with the heat of the spray. He felt cold down to the bone, and nothing could possibly warm him again except the touch of the one woman he would always love.

Clad in only a towel, he fell back onto his bed, imagining the sky beyond his ceiling as if it contained the answers he so desperately sought.

Till was so close, physically, just a floor below in her bedroom, and usually he could sense her presence just as clearly as one feels the sunlight streaming in through a window on a spring morning. He couldn't feel it as much any longer, and that was something more that made him wonder.

Was their connection in all things fading because of the space he'd been forced to put between them for her own good? Could her memory lapses have anything to do with any of it, or were they unrelated?

Would he be able to tolerate the separation, that loss of the comfort of her mind constantly beside

his, ready to respond any moment he reached out for it?

He had to question in this moment, who was putting more space between them these days. She certainly was trying harder at it, and he still wished he knew why. After all, she had no memory of the passionate night they'd spent in each other's arms. Even if she still had feelings for him, she shouldn't feel as strong a need to pull away from him as he did from her.

She wasn't burdened with the knowledge of things that they couldn't change, but had both so desperately wished to.

Gus was grateful for that. The thought of her possibly remembering, somehow, was devastating. He could handle the pain on his own behalf — at least, most of the time he felt he could — but if he ever knew that she was suffering and that he was the cause of it... or rather, the lack of his love was the cause of it... he didn't know how he'd keep from crumbling and telling her everything, all over again.

His mind wandered back to the paper that Till had written the year before, about the future of Fairy Godparents and how unions between them were going to have to not only be acceptable, but mandatory in the future if the species was to be saved from eventual extinction. How Gus wished that he and Till could be a test case for such an endeavor. He considered how powerful their love had been when shared, just that one night, and he wondered how something so vital, something that made him feel so much more alive than he ever had, could possibly pose a danger to anyone.

Then he remembered the danger— punishment. The fate his parents had suffered, which had ended in calamity for their family.

Now Gus was the last of his line, and feared it would die along with him. Even if hundreds of years from now, it seemed all too soon to erase the names Duncan and O'Sullivan from their storied history among Fairy Godparents.

He closed his eyes and wished, in vain, for sleep. He could still remember how it felt to drift off, especially on nights when you were lucky enough not to dream at all. Time would pass, morning would come, and things never seemed quite as bad after a solid night's rest.

Now what passed for rest never seemed to buoy his spirits or change his point of view. Things appeared as dark in the morning as they had in the moonlight, and the memory of her kiss was just as fresh as the moment she had first placed it upon his lips. Sweet, warm, and evocative, it was all the things she was; everything he never even knew he wanted before they met.

He longed for her, and no amount of wishing it away was going to make him feel less lonely for her this night.

Chapter Seventeen
The Scare

GUS WAS STILL IN BED in the early morning hours of the next day, resting his eyes and trying not to think, when he heard a clear, piercing sound inside his head.

It was akin to a telepathic scream, and caused him to leap up and throw on his clothing as quickly as he could.

He appeared in Till's kitchen with his shirt still half undone. She stood before the sink, shaking furiously. She had gone completely pale, and it took Gus only a moment to ascertain why. Something had gone terribly wrong with Emma.

"Put on yer shoes," he said. "I'll start the truck."

She barely nodded, her face a portrait of fear and despair. As he threw on his leather jacket he was already dialing his cell phone, ready to tell Mrs. Nesbitt that they were going to run a little behind this morning.

He rushed outside and went around the front of the truck to open Till's door for her. She dashed out of the house with only a sweater over her shoulders and no idea she'd forgotten her purse.

Gus tilted his head and gazed at her with great affection. "Oh, Tilda Mae," he whispered, and a moment later she was wearing the coat and holding her purse in her lap.

"What would I do without you?" she whispered, tears brimming and threatening to spill.

He placed his hand on top of hers for a moment before he was forced to pull it back. The warmth and chemistry between them was unmistakable, and unbearable, even with so slight a touch. "I promise, ye'll never have to find out."

He threw the truck into gear and kicked up gravel as he sped down Finch Street. "Any idea what the trouble is?"

"I'm not sure. I tried to get an impression but I could only feel her fear," Till replied, catching her bottom lip between her teeth and holding it there a moment before going on. "She's afraid and wished for me. That's all I know."

"We'll have to find Dianne," Gus instructed, knowing that Till was far too preoccupied to think of a plan of action. Everything inside of her was just telling her that she needed to get to Emma, but they had to be cautious how they went about doing it. The child may understand exactly what Till was, but no one else did.

* * *

"Go in there and come out in uniform," Gus instructed, once they'd arrived. He gently pushed Till toward the ladies' room. "I'll change and meet ye here."

He went into the men's restroom and emerged in his janitorial disguise. This time he decided to forgo the mop and pail of water, carrying only a spray bottle of cleaning solution and a rag. He threaded the end of the cloth through his belt and was quickly on his way.

In a few moments that seemed to stretch an eternity, he found Till again and took her aside. He decided to risk taking the same elevator this time, thinking better of letting her out of his sight in the condition she was in. Within moments they were in the hallway of the children's cardiac floor.

He sighted Dianne and locked eyes with her as they approached. "Take extra care with room 4311..." Dianne said loudly as a group of doctors walked past. Gus nodded.

The moment they were alone, Dianne glanced across the hallway at Till and motioned for her to wait before going into Emma's room. She looked puzzled as she stared in Till's direction, and Gus was surprised to find Dianne's thoughts projected into his head a second later.

She's not supposed to have any visitors, Dianne explained to Gus, who opened up his thoughts enough so that Till could hear every word from where she stood down the hall. *I'll have to go in and draw* the curtains to take her vitals. Till can pop in and out, literally, but she can't stay. Still, I think it will do the child an immense amount of good to see her.

All right, Gus thought, and he nodded to Till. He observed her confusion and sighed. "I'm not sure she got any of that. I'll have to have a word."

"Do it *quickly*," Dianne warned. "If they catch Till breaking a no visitors rule, they'll fire her."

"Got it." Gus moved quickly down the hall, caught Till's gaze, and then gestured with his eyes toward a small empty room marked 'family waiting'. He went inside and a second later, she followed.

"Did ye get all that?"

"I don't think so." Till shook her head as if trying to clear it. The corners of her mouth turned downward. "I just heard 'no visitors', but Gus, I've got to see her. I know it will help."

"This is what we have to do…" She watched him closely, but Gus was certain that she still wasn't really hearing him. "Tilda Mae, ye've got to listen now, yeah?"

"Sorry, sorry." She shook her head again. "All I can feel is her fear and it's breaking my heart."

"Ye'll help to put that right," Gus promised. "But ye have to sneak in, and ye can only stay so long as it takes Dianne to check her vitals. Ye have to appear in the room and then disappear directly from it. No walkin' in or out. Understand?"

"No walking in or out. Got it."

"Meet me in the parking lot by the truck, just be sure no one sees ye comin' or goin'."

"Okay."

Gus reluctantly left her side, spraying down the handrails in the hallway with cleaner and wiping the moisture away. He tried to hear what was happening in the room but only got bits and pieces from Till, as her thoughts wound up and spun in an erratic frenzy. His own powers seemed to be less than cooperative now; his mind like a radio, trying to reach a signal broken apart by distance and static. He couldn't make sense of the noise. He was having such a hard time that he actually resorted to asking for help.

Dianne, is there anythin' ye can do for me here?

I'll try my best, Gus… she thought back to him, and opened her mind up to Gus as she very slowly, very carefully, checked the child's vitals... refilled her water cup... offered her a drink... anything and everything she could do to stall to give Till more time in the room.

With Dianne's assistance, Gus was finally able to get a good read on what was happening.

Till had disappeared into the nearest empty elevator and then popped up in Emma's room. Emma was thrilled to see her, though she seemed groggy and out of it.

"Till!" the little girl tried to exclaim, but her voice was hoarse. "I wished you would come."

"I'm here, sweetheart, I'm here..." Till's thoughts next questioned Dianne, and Dianne answered quickly.

She spiked a fever a little while ago and they feared post-op infection. She's on IV antibiotics as a precaution and we're still trying to keep the fever down. They also gave her a mild sedative because she was so terrified.

"I can't stay long, Emma," Till whispered. "I just wanted to come by to tell you that I'm thinking of you, and I will visit you again as soon as I can. As soon as they allow visitors back in your room, or you go home. Okay?"

"I dreamed that you would come," Emma mumbled. "They made me leave Remington home. I miss him."

"I know, but you have to be brave for me, okay? Just wait a little while longer and you'll be back home with Remington in no time. Can you be brave for me?"

"I... think so." Emma closed her eyes, drifting off once more.

Time's up, Till, Dianne thought.

"I have to go now... but I will see you soon. You're going to be just fine, do you hear me? Just fine..."

"I... love you, Till," Emma whispered, and then she curled small fingers around her blanket and succumbed to sleep.

Till nodded her thanks to Dianne, and then disappeared from the room.

When she met up with Gus at the truck they were both back in their street clothes, and she was, once again, crying. She spent so much time crying lately, Gus really wished that he could do something to console her or better still, prevent the need for tears.

"She's going to be all right, Tilda Mae," Gus said, as he put the key into the Chevy's ignition and turned it. "I promise ye that."

* * *

After they arrived back at the house, the pair sat in silence at the kitchen table, holding on to their empty teacups and thinking only of the little girl they had left behind at the hospital.

Gus didn't know what would happen to Till if things didn't turn out all right, and he hoped his promise would hold.

Till jumped as her phone rang inside her purse. She grabbed it and answered immediately, recognizing the number on the screen. "Dianne?"

Gus watched Till's shoulders relax as she sank back into her chair. "Thank you so much. See you later."

She tossed the phone onto the table and looked up at him. She nodded, tears in her eyes and a smile on her face; an expression that needed no explanation. The danger had passed, and Emma was going to be fine.

* * *

Gus left Till shortly after the good news had come, and with their schedules at the store in conflict, didn't see her again until the next night.

He came around the corner with his broom in his hand, approaching her on the porch. "Evenin', Till. Am I disturbin' you?" Part of him hoped that he was, that maybe he could get her to talk about whatever was going on inside of her that kept her such a mystery to him these days.

"Not at all," Till answered from her perch upon the porch swing. "If you want to sweep, sweep."

He nodded and did just so, moving the broom in slow, deliberate motions as Till's gaze upon him seemed to fade off into the distance.

She was staring through him, and he was left to wonder, as he was so often lately, exactly what she was really thinking.

The surface thoughts were there for him to pick up on, sure enough. It was *a lovely evening, the sky was myriad shades of blue, with the stars just starting to come out,* that kind of thing. But there was so much more, he knew, always hiding beneath that superficial flurry of activity.

He watched as her feet moved to and fro against the porch, propelling the swing to go faster. Her toes barely touched the ground in those silly, grand, rubber-toed high top shoes. Her skirt swung against her legs and then flew free of them, though it was too long to reveal any of the soft skin beneath.

God, how I miss her skin...

"Want to sit down?" she asked, as Gus continued to putter nearby with his broom, sweeping little bits of mostly imaginary dust back onto the driveway.

"No, thanks."

She looked at him sideways. "Having trouble holding still tonight?"

He shrugged.

"Me too." She raised her hands up to her sides, parting her fingers, feeling the rush of the air between them as the swing swished forward and back. "I miss having a real swing, like at the schoolyard when I was a kid. On those, you could almost fly."

Gus knew he shouldn't, really, but in this moment he couldn't stop himself. He made the slightest of gestures with his hand and then pointed toward the largest tree in the yard. "Like that one?"

Till stared for a long moment before she believed what she was seeing. He'd hung a large wooden swing from the tree's sturdiest bough.

"No way!" Till skidded to a halt on the porch swing and took off toward the tree. "Come *on*, Gus!" she called after him, but he hesitated. If she wanted him to push her up high, as he imagined she would, that would mean touching her, even if only on the back or shoulders. Touching her would stir feelings in him that he continued to battle, hidden from her of necessity.

In this moment, he wasn't sure how to get out of the situation without making himself look suspicious no matter what he did.

It was so good to see her truly smiling, even if just for a second. He leaned the broom up against the wall and followed her out onto the lawn.

She was already swinging a little, pumping her arms against the ropes to gain momentum.

Sure enough, she shouted, "Give me a push!", sounding like an excited child but looking nothing at all like one.

"Tilda Mae..."

"C'mon! Just a couple of good ones?"

Gus sighed. He took up position behind her and when she came toward him, he reached out. A thought occurred to him suddenly, and he stopped before he actually touched her.

With another small gesture of his hand, she picked up speed and swung higher.

"Hey, that's cheating!" Till said, looking back at him. "You sweep the old fashioned way. Just give me a regular push!"

Gus shored up his mental fields with images of anything random he could begin to think of, and then extended his arms and pressed his hands against her back, sending her forward again.

She threw her head backwards and laughed; the most beautiful, heartrending laugh Gus had ever heard in his life. For a moment, the only ropes in her life were the ones her fingers were wrapped around. There was nothing tying her down; no restrictions on her other than the inevitable return back toward level ground as gravity dictated.

Her thoughts were open and welcoming to him, as she used the force he'd applied to full benefit, stretching out her legs and pointing her toes to fly ever higher.

"Careful, now," Gus warned, a little worried. He had no concerns about the sturdiness of the swing, only that she might somehow let go and fall too far.

He'd already *fallen too far,* and he didn't know how he was going to spend the rest of his life living with it.

Her mind snapped shut, and he winced. The sensation was physically painful for him, like a jab in the ribs, every time it happened.

She slowly wound her momentum down, dragging her toes against the lawn as she'd brush past. Gus looked up at her, concerned, and helped slow her by grasping the ropes a moment before releasing them as she'd go by.

"Everythin' all right?"

"I'm a little dizzy," Till said, as she finally came to a stop and looked at him again. "I think I got carried away." She tried to rise on unsteady feet, and teetered. Gus rushed forward to catch her before she could fall, and she met his eyes with a stare so vacant that it chilled him clear through.

"Need any help getting back?"

"No." Her voice was small and ragged. "I can make it on my own."

Then she was gone, and Gus felt a far too familiar longing. He knew better than to follow her.

He slumped down onto the swing, grasped hold of the ropes still warm from her touch, and stayed there a good long while.

Chapter Eighteen
Home

A WEEK PASSED SINCE TILL HAD SEEN EMMA, and she seemed barely able to hold still as she spoke. She wrung her hands as she glanced at Emma's house nearby, and adjusted the shoulders on her sweater again and again. She finally gave up on trying to get them to stay straight. "I'm so nervous, I really hope she doesn't pick up on it."

"It'll be all right, ye'll see. Just keep yer mind on why y'er there and she'll be so happy to see ye that ye won't believe it."

"Yeah, but this is the first time I'm going to see a charge who *knows* I'm a Fairy Godmother. Well, at least when she's not heavily sedated." Till swayed a little from side to side, causing her skirt to twirl around her legs. She looked adorable in this moment, and Gus had to fight the urge to hug her close. "Should I change into something... poofier?"

"Poofier?" he asked, tilting his head to the side.

"You know... poofier!" She held her skirt out at the edges and then gestured widely. "More like a pageant contestant, or refugee from Oz."

Gus laughed softly. "No need. Just be yourself, Tilda Mae. That's who she's wishin' to see right now."

"Can I bring a friend along?"

"For the first time, I think it's best if ye go in alone, but I'll be just out here, so."

"So." Till sighed, and finally stopped stalling. "Okay. But if her parents catch me I'm going to blame it on you not being in there to pull me out."

"Be careful," Gus warned, his heart speeding up a bit. It was always riskier going on a visit when the charge knew who you were, especially the young children, because if they did shout in excitement at your arrival, you had to be ready to hide or transport in a hurry, and would be forced to leave the charge looking like they had imagined the whole thing, which was something Gus loathed.

He had thought it prudent that he drive them to Emma's house tonight, since he needed somewhere to hide and his truck seemed the safest location. He ducked down a little in the seat, pretending to stare at the screen on his phone, which he never actually bothered to turn on, and waited. He tuned into Till's thoughts and found that he could visualize the room, and the girl, with great clarity.

Till was hiding in the closet.

She waited a moment, seemingly frozen. She thought she heard Emma talking to someone, and it took her a moment to realize that it was only the teddy bear that Till had given her.

"Ready for sleep, Remington?" Emma asked sounding a little sad. "Good. You got your bandage on? Okay. Your heart is gonna be better in no time." Her voice dropped down low. "You know, I thought that maybe she would come visit us tonight... but I guess not."

Till, that's yer cue... Gus thought.

Cue? Oh! Right!

Till knocked very softly on the inside of the closet door, then opened it just an inch. "Emma?" she whispered.

Emma gasped and looked up. "You did come! You did!" Emma said excitedly, and both Till and Gus cringed as from the next room they heard a stern, male voice tell Emma to settle down and go to sleep.

"Okay Daddy," Emma replied, gesturing for Till to come out from hiding. "You kept your promise!"

"I try my best to keep my promises, Emma," Till said, finally allowing herself to gently touch the child's hair. Emma patted the bed beside her.

"Please, sit with me. Just for a little bit."

"I better not stay long on my first visit, but okay." As soon as she sat, she was shocked by the speed and ferocity with which little arms encircled her.

"I'm sooooo happy to see you," Emma said, squeezing hard.

"Careful, careful, honey, not too tight now. I don't want to hurt you."

"I'm okay," Emma said, smiling up at Till with absolute adoration. "You promised that I was going to be okay, and I am. You were right about that, too."

"I kept an eye on you, you know," Till whispered. "My heart is always with you, Emma. And if you ever really need me, if you wish me here, I will always do my very best to get here."

"That's a very special wish," Emma declared solemnly. "I better save it for when it's important."

Gus thought his heart would melt at the sight playing out inside his head so clearly... that of Till gently rocking Emma in her arms, and Emma clutching her teddy bear. Seeing Till with a child again rendered Gus weak, and he had to fight once more to keep the wishes within him from threatening to surface... wishes for things that could never be.

"It doesn't always have to be important," Till said, as she tenderly smoothed down Emma's hair. "Just know that if you wish for me, I might not be able to come right then. It might take a little while. But I promise to do my best, and I hope you'll promise me something."

"What?"

"That you'll remember that no matter how lonely you might feel sometimes, that you're not ever really alone. You have a Fairy Godmother now, and I will be watching over you."

"I love you, Till."

Gus felt a lump lodge in his throat; equal to the one that rose up in Till's.

"I love you too, Emma."

Gus felt the pang in Till's heart as she slowly extricated herself from the child's grasp. "You need to get your rest now, okay?" She tucked the covers in and gave the teddy bear a little pat on the nose before she turned to go.

"Till?"

"Hmm?"

"Can I have one more hug?"

Till's throat ached with the sting of unshed tears, Gus knew, because suddenly he could feel that as a physical sensation, too.

Till nodded to Emma and returned to her bedside, leaning down to give her a gentle, loving hug. Then she kissed the top of the girl's head. "You're never alone, Emma. Remember."

"I will. Good night, Till."

"Good night."

Till appeared beside Gus in the truck a moment later, and he was swept under by the wave of overwhelming, conflicting emotions emanating from her. She was struggling for control of them, but losing the battle. She was shaken, and trembling, and after a moment she dropped her head into her hands.

Gus wanted to help her, but didn't know how. Her thoughts were impossible to make sense of, and as before, the experience frightened him. He started up the truck and drove around the block before parking it, concerned that if they stayed where they were any longer they'd draw unwanted attention.

"Tilda Mae, what is it?" he asked, attempting to pull her hands away from her face.

She looked at him, heartache distorting her sweet features. He felt a deep ache in his chest; her sorrow was, in this moment, again his. His stomach clenched and he felt as though he might be sick.

Then just as quickly as the pain had risen in her, it was gone.

Gus gasped sharply, his mind and body thrown into a state of utter confusion.

"What?" She asked, clearly bewildered. "Where are we?"

"We were just out on a visit," he said, knowing better by this point than to think that she was making some kind of joke. Still, he had to be certain. "Don't you remember?"

"What are you talking about? Who were we visiting?" She paused, thinking. "Oh wait, I know. We dropped off that book my mom wanted to borrow from the library?"

Gus was near total panic now. "You really don't remember?"

"What am I supposed to remember?"

"Emma!" Gus exclaimed, so terrified that he just blurted the name out. "Yer charge, the wee one from the hospital! She's home now and we just went to make sure she was okay. She's fine but y'er the one that is scarin' the life outta me, Tilda Mae."

"Gus, what are you going on about? I don't know anyone named Emma. Why would I be at a hospital, let alone visiting some child that I met there? You're not making any sense."

"No, Till, yer the one who is not makin' sense," Gus took hold of her by the arms. "I can't read yer thoughts now. Why can't I read yer thoughts?"

"Read my... what the hell are you talking about?" Till was not only getting angry, but she looked truly frightened. "Is that some sort of joke? I know that we know each other well by this point, but to be able to actually read my thoughts you'd have to be some kind of..."

A Fairy Godfather could do it, Gus thought to her, testing to see if she could still hear him even though he couldn't read her now.

He waited a seeming eternity... there was no response.

"You are making absolutely no sense tonight," Till said, huffing as she wrenched herself free of his grasp. "I don't care where we've been or where we were going, take me home."

"Till, listen to me, please. Somethin's goin' wrong here, we have got to figure out what it is."

"Take. Me. Home. Now." She demanded. "Or else I will get out and walk."

"It's gonna rain, and is not safe for ye to be out alone so late..."

"Then please, Gus," her voice broke as she begged now. "Just take me home."

"All right."

She rocked back and forth anxiously in her seat the whole drive. Then, as they turned on to Finch Street and headed up the long driveway, she slowly stopped.

"Emma is so sweet," she said softly.

In a moment of confusion Gus floored the accelerator, and nearly drove his truck into her parked car from the shock of the sudden onslaught of her thoughts reentering his mind. Then he slammed on the brakes. *"What?"*

"Emma," Till said, blinking repeatedly. "You know, the little kid we just got done visiting? She's such a little angel. If I could have kids, I'd want a dozen like her."

"Till... wait. Let me get this right, because I think am losin' my mind," Gus stammered. "Ye remember Emma now?"

"How could I forget Emma?"

"Ye forgot Emma *fifteen minutes ago* and continued to have *no memory of her until this very second!*" Gus's voice rose with his frustration, but he fought to keep it even. "Scared me near to death, Tilda Mae, ye did, and it's not the first time either. Has anyone else noticed any problems with yer memory?"

The thought jumped into Till's mind that her mother had scolded her several times at the store in the past week for forgetting what she was supposed to be doing and starting on another task, but Till did not speak the truth aloud.

"I knew it!" Gus slapped the steering wheel. "There is something seriously wrong happenin' here, and I'm worried about ye, Till. Truly worried. We... have to talk to someone about this."

"There's nothing to talk to anyone about," Till insisted, opening the door to the truck instead of waiting for Gus to come around and do it for her. "I'm fine." She sounded unconvinced though, even as she spoke the words; and for the moment remained where she sat.

"Y'er nowhere NEAR fine!" Gus cried, running a hand back through his hair and then leaning his head down against the steering wheel. "Tilda Mae, I'm tellin' ye, there are times when I can read ye so clearly now that I can see what is goin' on all around ye at the time. Like tonight, in Emma's room. Was like watchin' a bloody movie. I could see *everything*."

Till said nothing in response.

A crack of thunder pierced the night sky, which finally opened up in a downpour.

"I could visualize it, Till. It's not the first time I've had images flash through my mind with such clarity. It's like we're so far into each other's heads now that... Till, wait!"

She jumped down out of the truck and headed for the porch in the driving rain.

Gus ran after her and grasped hold of her by the shoulders as they stood there, getting soaked.

"STAY OUT OF MY HEAD!" Till cried, pushing his hands away. Her mind was skipping from thought to thought so quickly that Gus could not understand them now. "I DON'T WANT YOU IN THERE!"

"Tilda Mae, please, let me help..."

"Want to help? LEAVE ME ALONE!" Till flicked her wrist and the front door flew open. She ran inside and slammed it, leaving Gus alone in the rain, up against the battlements between their minds once more.

Chapter Nineteen
Running Away

GUS ROSE FROM HIS BED after another expected sleepless night, feeling no better than he had when he'd climbed into it.

He dressed and considered the idea of eating, but knew he couldn't do it. Even the thought of coffee was distasteful. He tried to shake the fog from his head but failed miserably.

He didn't know what he needed at this point, though he was sorely aware of what he wanted. What he wanted had never changed; not since the instant that something flipped inside of him and he started also needing it.

Since he could not have it —have *her* — whether it be need or want, his emotions ate at him slowly, day by day. The more Till pulled away, the worse it felt. At least when he was able to feel like her best friend, he could somehow convince himself that someday things could be different between them. That a miracle might happen, or some other unlikely but desperately wished for event would make things between them possible.

"I am going to go mad if I don't go somewhere," Gus thought aloud. "Far away." He needed to do something drastic to put distance between him and the situation he found himself in, for at least a few days. He needed to do something different. He needed to do something *human*.

He reached for the cell phone that sat on the bedside table and hit speed dial. A youthful voice answered.

"Ryan? Yeah... it's Gus. How are ye, lad? Glad to hear it. And yer ma? Right, that's grand. Listen, Ryan, I know I promised to come to see ye and haven't yet. I know this is kind of short notice but I was wonderin' if ye'd be up for a visit this weekend? Yes, I know it's Friday already. I'm thinkin' of flyin' standby on the next flight out and… no, no, wouldn't dream of it, I'll stay in a hotel. Is yer ma there? Would ye ask her if it would be all right, please?"

Gus waited impatiently, thinking that even if he couldn't see Ryan and his mother this weekend, he was still going to take an old fashioned trip, no fairy powers involved, somewhere south in an attempt to find the sun.

"She has to work? It's all right, maybe we can go to dinner… before that we can just hang out… sure, I'm glad too. It's settled then. I'll call ye before I come over… right. See ye then."

He closed the connection and then flipped open his laptop. He really was determined to plan and take this trip in the way that he would if he were 100% human, checked baggage charges and all.

He booked his flight and rental car, and then a hotel room, at a place right on the beach near Tampa Bay. He needed to tread unfamiliar sand, to put the heartache behind him for only a moment, if he could.

Making the reservations was the easy part; the hard part would be calling off from work for the weekend. Sometimes he wondered how much longer he'd be able to stay on at Happily Ever After Books. Maybe if he didn't have to spend all day with Till while they worked, and then also in their second life as Fairy Godparents… but then he realized he was only kidding himself. Wherever he was, she was always going to be on his mind.

He went to the closet and pulled out the suitcase he hadn't used since he came to live in America — the old fashioned way, also, by plane — before he'd taken control of the powers that were rising inside of him. They were an angry tide that nearly drowned him, and may have, if not for the kindness of old Aunt Tilda.

The sight of that suitcase took him back to a time he'd rather forget, and he felt sad thinking just how much of his life he wished he could erase from memory.

He set the suitcase on the bed and unlatched it, opened a drawer, and began to pack. Halfway through the task, he took his phone up again and dialed; it was time to face the music.

"Missus, it's Gus. I hate to ask so late, but I really need the weekend — no, not really *sick*, just, I need to take care of something important, and I won't be able to make it in. I know, I'm sorry. I'm sure that Till and Amber can handle that… or leave it, and I'll handle it first thing when I get back. I promise to trade shifts with anyone next week who wants to, to make up for it… I really appreciate it, Missus, thank ye. No, I'll be fine, don't worry about me. All right. Thanks again."

Gus allowed himself to flop back onto the bed for a moment, feeling completely worn out by the exchange. His head throbbed and his eyes hurt, but not as much as his heart.

It was going to take all of his resolve, and all of his powers, to keep Till out when she inevitably tried to find and follow him. He had no doubt that she would; after all, if the situation were reversed and she disappeared for days without a word to him, he'd search the world high and low until he found her. Still, he felt he'd come unhinged if he didn't get some time away, alone. He had to do this.

He was counting heavily on the fact that he had more experience than she did, even though she was becoming so incredibly powerful it defied all expectation.

She had no idea just how powerful she was yet; and in a way, Gus hoped she never would. Underestimating her powers may slow her down a little, but it kept her safely, and endearingly, humble.

Soon he was on his way to the airport, parking his truck, making his way to the check-in kiosk. He proceeded through security. His only carry-on was a small black backpack; he had checked his suitcase in an attempt to feel as light on the journey as possible. There was little point, though, he soon discovered. The weight was tying him to earth with such force he feared the plane may not be able to take off with him on it. It felt buried deep in the left side of his chest.

He tried not to think of Till, to the point where he actually got out his old MP3 player — which he used only as a prop when in public in order to look like everybody else, since he could recall every piece of music he'd ever heard in perfect clarity inside of his head anytime he wanted to. He tried using it not only in an attempt to mask the noise in his own mind, but as a gigantic "Do Not Disturb" sign for the rest of the world.

Being a Fairy Godparent was all about helping, and Gus certainly wasn't about to let the elderly woman in front of him in line struggle with her heavy bag alone. Aside from that random act of kindness, though, he had no desire to interact with anyone on the journey. He wanted to be as alone as he could be, and if that meant artificially crafted solitude, then so be it.

He paced the floor near the gate until he began to draw suspicious stares from airline personnel passing by. He forced himself to sit down, to try to calm down, but nothing would quell the storm inside him.

He stared at his boarding pass for the hundredth time. He'd booked his ticket so late his seat was at the back of the plane. By the time he struggled into it he found himself sitting in the center seat between a couple that was in the middle of a heated exchange.

"I can't believe you left it home," the man said with an exaggerated sigh.

"I was so sure that it was in my purse…" the woman replied, averting her eyes from his withering stare. She delved into the depths of her handbag, so huge that it lopped over the side of the armrest and halfway into Gus's lap.

"You must have left it in the bedroom. I checked the kitchen counters and table before we left." The man answered, continuing to glare at her. "I can't believe it. The new camera the kids got us last Christmas, now it's just going to sit there continuing to gather dust instead of going on our trip with us. I don't know how you can be so empty headed."

The woman stared at her lap, dejected, and blinked back tears as she continued looking through her purse, but much more slowly now.

Gus couldn't stand to listen to the man berating his wife. He wished he could do so much more for the woman than simply to make the camera appear so that the current tirade would stop; but that was all he could do, and so he did it.

In an instant when she closed her purse for a moment, Gus delved deep enough into her thoughts to find, and retrieve, her camera, which had actually fallen out when they went through security.

"It can't help to keep looking in there, you've done it a hundred… times…" The man's words slowed, as the woman gasped in triumph. She reached into her bag one last time and pulled out the missing camera.

Gus suppressed his reaction at seeing how happy it made her and leaned back in his seat, closing his eyes as if ready to take a nap.

Mission accomplished, he thought. *Now maybe we can all have some quiet.*

Gus knew that it was also self-serving to have retrieved the misplaced item for the total stranger, but he just couldn't stand the thought of listening to the man rant the entire way to Florida.

"Well, would you look at that," she said, nudging Gus's arm in an attempt to get his attention. Gus barely opened his eyes to look at her. "It was in my purse the whole time, after all."

Gus smiled politely, then pretended to turn up the volume on his MP3 player, before closing his eyes again and leaning back against the seat. His arms were bent awkwardly across his lap, as he struggled for real estate in the tiny row of airline seats.

Several more times the woman tried to start a conversation, but her attempts fell flat, mostly because he never took out his earbuds. Though he could hear her just fine with them in, he desperately hoped she'd get the point that he really just wanted to be left alone. Finally an idea occurred to him.

"Would ye like to switch seats with me, Missus? So that ye and yer husband can sit together?"

"Heavens no!" She looked horrified at the thought. "I like things *just the way they are.*"

The plane taxied for what seemed forever down the tarmac, before the engines finally revved and Gus felt the power of the aircraft kick in. The force pressed him back into his seat, and he fought against its pull to look forward, watching out the window past the gentleman blocking most of it as the ground disappeared beneath and the plane headed up and into a bank of smoke gray clouds.

The higher they rose, the whiter the clouds became, and Gus enjoyed letting the sight of them fill his mind and mix with the music playing in his ears until the moment that the man in the window seat decided he'd had enough of the view and unceremoniously slammed the shade shut.

Gus leaned back, once more feigning sleep. He longed desperately for the real thing, and wondered why he hadn't just done things the easy way and transported himself from one location to the other, skipping the flight entirely.

But then, that would have been cheating, he thought. He wanted the human experience for this trip, he was going to have it — the good, the bad, and the annoying.

No matter how he tried to stop it, his mind kept returning to Till. Reviewing the time he had known her in his head like a film of his life, a story that really began the moment he met her and had gone on from there. Nothing much that happened before that day seemed to have any significance to him now; at least, nothing that wasn't to do with his family or where he'd come from. He still felt wounded whenever he considered his parents and their fate… something that became more embedded in his consciousness with each passing day.

He'd compared his parents' situation to his own and considered every possible scenario a million times. Every single time he'd come up with the same answer. If he did make any sort of attempt to hold Till's heart in this life, they would suffer his parents' fate.

Still, given the way that she'd gotten so much stronger since they'd been working together, a tiny part of him nagged at him, like a splinter in your hand you can't find. It remained fixed in his brain, that one thought, those two most dangerous words of all; whether thought, or written, or spoken.

What if…

Chapter Twenty
Arrival

OTHER THAN THE BARBS SHARED BETWEEN the man and woman on either side of him, and one moment of turbulence where he nearly ended up wearing the husband's beer, the flight was uneventful.

The moment he stepped onto the jet way he could feel the humidity, and it warmed his frozen bones in just the way he had hoped it might. He breathed in the heavy air, almost able to taste the change in climate from where he'd come.

It was a welcome sensation.

He made good time through baggage claim, slipping past hordes of befuddled tourists and returning Florida residents. Next he located the car rental counter. His car was waiting; a small white convertible that he never would have driven at home because it was just too impractical. Here, it seemed the perfect vehicle, if anything could be, in which he could take in the sun and try to soothe his broken heart.

He arrived at his beachside hotel and gave his keys to the valet. Though he had plans to see Ryan later in the day, school was still in session. Gus was looking forward to a little time alone to take in the sights and see if he could calm his nagging fears.

Suddenly he felt very far away from Till, even though he knew that, truthfully, he could close his eyes and think himself back to where she was in an instant. But he was trying to give her space, and trying to take some for himself as well. He was so engaged in using every ounce of his strength to keep her out of his thoughts in an attempt to find him that he was almost forced at this point to do everything else the old fashioned way. Every now and then, he'd hear a faint whisper in his mind, as though she was standing just over his shoulder and breathing the words into his ear.

Where are you?

He knew he dare not think back a single word in response, even if only to let her know he was okay. To tell her so would not only risk her honing in on the signal, but it would also be an outright lie. He wasn't okay, and he didn't believe he ever would be again. Not without her in his arms.

Gus moved slowly through the revolving door and shivered as the air in the temperature controlled lobby met his skin. He'd baked in the sun on the drive in from the airport; to meet the cold again so suddenly was a shock to his system.

He was arriving off-hours, after check-out time but before standard check-in, so there was no one waiting at the counter when he approached.

"Welcome!" a soft, friendly voice greeted him as he took out his driver's license and credit card to prove his identity. "Who might this be?"

Still not feeling like speaking, Gus simply pushed the cards over the counter toward the hotel employee.

"Mr. Angus Duncan... my, isn't that an exotic name. It says that you've booked the standard view room here... is that correct?"

Gus sighed. Apparently he was going to have to talk, though he sensed that the woman was only pressing because she wanted to know if his accent matched his name. "Aye."

"Oh!" She squealed like a schoolgirl and batted her eyelashes. "Are you from *Scotland*?"

"I'm actually from Detroit," Gus replied, completely straight faced.

"Oh," she said again, this time sounding disappointed.

He sighed deeply. "But before I lived there, I grew up in the UK."

"Oh!" The word once again took on a happy excitement as she rubbed her hands together. "So it was Scotland, then?"

"Scotland and Ireland, both, and can I see about my room key, please? Been a long trip."

"Of course... well you know you're here before check-in time, but let me see if any of the rooms are ready..." She typed incessantly and then scanned her computer screen with squinted eyes. She smiled, tapped a few more keys, and then moved to a small machine beside her. She inserted what looked like a blank credit card emblazoned with the hotel chain's logo on it and coded his room key. "Well, I'm sorry Mr. Duncan, but we didn't have availability in the standard room you requested. There is a large wedding party at the hotel this weekend, you know what happens, they underbook and then we need to move things around..."

"Whatever view you have will be acceptable," Gus said, though minor annoyance crept through in his voice. He thought standard was the basic view... what the view was going to be beyond that, he didn't know and was too tired to care.

"I think you'll like this room. Enjoy your stay, and if you need anything... please, and I do mean please, feel free to come back to the desk and ask for me."

"Thank ye kindly... Marsha," he said, reading her name badge.

She giggled again when he said her name. "Or just call and ask for me..."

"Thanks, I'll remember that." He tucked his key and cards into his wallet and turned away.

"Wait! You forgot your welcome packet! And your chocolate chip cookie!"

Gus paused. "Cookie?"

"Everyone gets a cookie when they check in."

His stomach flipped at the thought of food. "Thank ye, but no."

"But everyone loves the cookie!"

Gus sighed again. "Will take the packet," he offered, some small consolation.

She smiled and pushed a folder across the counter. Gus nodded and swept it up, tucking it under his arm as he grabbed his suitcase and adjusted his backpack. "Thanks again."

"Remember, I work all weekend!" She called after him as he headed toward the elevator. "Call if you need *anything at all*!"

* * *

The moment Gus stepped into his room and moved toward the balcony, he saw why Marsha had said he would enjoy the view.

She had given him a considerable upgrade. His room faced the beach and the Gulf of Mexico beyond; a shoreline so clear and beautiful that he couldn't wait to walk along it.

Till would love this, he thought, and just as quickly as his spirits had lifted a little, they sank.

How he would have loved to bring her here, or somewhere just like it, for a proper honeymoon…

He opened his suitcase and took out his leather jacket, which he had crammed into it somewhere between baggage claim and the car rental counter, and hung it up in the closet. He thought about unpacking everything, but then decided not to waste the time.

He left the suitcase closed on the stand at the bottom of the king sized bed with perfectly arranged piles of pillows on it. Pillows that begged to be thrown aside, blankets twisted and abandoned in the heat of passion…

His mind returned to New Year's Eve and he groaned. No matter where he was, he couldn't escape her memory.

He walked over to the glass door and slid it open, stepping out onto the balcony. Down on the beach below were rows of sunbathers and people splashing in the surf; many of them scantily clad women. None of them caught or held his interest, however. His heart belonged to only one woman, a woman who was probably clutching her coat closer around her as she stood in the freezing rain that had refused to turn into the expected light showers of spring.

He felt guilty, now, leaving her behind, but there was no way he could have brought her along. It was difficult enough for him to behave himself when the weather and scenery were much less welcoming; what might he have done if he'd brought her to a tropical paradise?

"Stop! Just stop!" he exclaimed, holding his head in his hands.

Maybe the less time he spent in the beautifully appointed, romantically decorated hotel room, the better.

He grabbed his sunglasses out of the breast pocket of his jacket and put them on.

He never wore shorts or heaven forbid, sandals, so still in a t-shirt, boots, and jeans, he headed for the hallway, closed the door behind him, and sought out the elevator once more.

It was time for a walk on that beach.

* * *

He stepped up to the tiki bar and looked at the people around him, all drinking frosty, fruity concoctions. He had an overwhelming craving for a chocolate milkshake, but knew he dare not indulge. He had to pick Ryan up later on and take him out to dinner; there was no way he'd ever even have one potentially intoxicating drink and risk driving.

So instead he ordered something the taste of which would soothe his soul and the effects of which were lost entirely on Fairy Godparents: alcohol.

"What can I get ya, sweetheart?" The female bartender asked, giving Gus a quick once-over as she did so.

He pointed to the tap of his choice. "Just a pint of that, please and thank ye."

"Sure thing." She pulled the tap and filled a glass. "You must have just come in from up North," she added, setting his beer down before him.

Gus tilted the glass to his lips and drank deeply. He took some money out of his wallet and tossed it onto the counter. "What makes ye say that?"

She leaned forward and lowered her voice. "Y'er ten shades of pale, and just a *wee bit* overdressed." She looked him up and downward again as she did her best to imitate his accent, and Gus shifted uncomfortably.

"Keep the change," he said as he turned away, prepared to take his beer with him on his walk.

"No glass allowed on the beach. They'll snatch it away from you before you can say 'lifeguard'. You may as well sit down."

Gus sighed, and finally sat.

She picked up a washrag and started wiping the counter around him. She moved away only long enough to wait on another patron, and then she turned her attention back to Gus, who had already finished his beer and was rising from his seat.

"Done already? You'd think that it had chocolate in it."

Gus paled even further. "What... did ye say?"

She leaned closer, her long, platinum blonde hair brushing against the counter as she did so. "I said, you'd think that you were drinking something chocolate, the way you finished that off so quickly."

Gus stared at her, perplexed. She smiled, and as she turned, prepared to cash out another customer, she added two words that left him reeling. "Nice bracelet."

Gus's eyes flew open wide. Only now did he observe her hands as they moved over the keys of the cash register, and noted that one was adorned by a ring that was very unique in a specific sort of way…

When she returned to him, she was grinning from ear to ear. "Bartending. Another job we get stuck with. Nights, weekends… holidays." She extended her hand toward him. "I'm Liz. It's nice to meet you, Gus."

Gus furrowed his brows. He was so engaged in trying to keep Till out of his head, was his mind really so open that his true identity was so obvious to anyone he may happen across who had an ounce of fairy in them?

"Don't be offended, please," she said, stepping back and holding her arms up in a gesture of surrender. "It's not like I was trying to read you. You just came in here projecting like IMAX."

Gus sat back down at the bar, averting his eyes.

"Besides, I'm a not an everyday, run-of-the-mill Fairy Godparent," she whispered now, leaning close. She was much too polite to try to invade his mental space by thinking the words to him.

He looked back up at her, appearing insulted by the term.

"I'm a helper!" she quickly explained. "Fairies in distress are my thing. I don't have charges… I'm kind of a fairy therapist. Specialized. Took me ten years of extra training at DCTU."

"Ten years?" Gus shook his head. "Ye must've sensed me comin' a mile away."

She looked at him sympathetically. "You're so tied up in knots, you have no idea how clear you were to me, the moment that you landed in Tampa. It's like a little signal goes off in my head, and I know that soon I'm going to meet someone who needs, at the very least, a safe ear to bend for a while."

"Thank ye kindly, but I won't be bendin' any ears today, or any other day. I should be on my way."

"You won't find the answer down there in the sand," she warned. "Or in the ocean or the sky above it. You won't find the answer anywhere but inside yourself, Angus Cailan Duncan." She took a few paces and started prepping lemons, cutting them into wedges on a small wooden board on the other side of the bar. "You might not even find it there, if you don't stop and listen to yourself long enough to hear it."

"Got to go," Gus said, rising again. He was thoroughly spooked now; he had to get away from this woman, whoever she was.

"If you really want me to leave you alone, I will, I promise. It's not my job to interfere, especially if people don't want to be helped."

He took a few unsteady steps forward, disoriented.

"However, I'm working days all weekend; you know what I do with my evenings," she said as he turned away. "If you change your mind and want to talk, I won't be hard to find."

Gus shuddered, wondering if anything in the world was ever a coincidence, or if he'd chosen this hotel from the many he could have picked because there was a helper here.

He had no intention of finding out just how good she might be at her job.

* * *

Gus meandered down toward the shore. It was habit, walking on the beach in his boots; though he wondered sometimes if he would find it more diverting if he did take them off and let the sand sift through his toes.

He had no desire to find out by trying it now. He was weary; too weary, he hated to admit, to bend over and untie the laces.

Despite the giggles and comments on his appearance from many a bikini clad woman in his wake, Gus trudged on. His shirt stuck to his skin in the humid air, and he wondered just how long he'd have to broil in the heat before he finally felt warm again.

He'd started to, just a little, but then this Liz woman appeared out of nowhere, and knew way too much about him right off the bat. It was nerve-wracking, and for once he wished there was a way to completely hide his fairy heritage from others of his kind, just for a little while.

By the time he reemerged from the ocean of his own thoughts, he realized that he needed to get a move on back to his room to clean up a bit. It was almost time to head over to pick up Ryan.

Chapter Twenty-One
Revelations

GUS DECIDED TO LET RYAN CHOOSE where he wanted to go for dinner, and the sky was the limit. It was nearly his seventeenth birthday, and Gus wanted him to mark the occasion with a proper celebration.

Ryan asked Gus to show him around his hotel; a sight that Ryan had only ever seen from the outside, and knew that he wouldn't be able to afford to see from the inside for many years to come.

With nothing but a gentle smile directed toward the girl at the podium, Gus was able to get them a table without a reservation. Not just any table either, but one overlooking the beach. Ryan's eyes grew to the size of the dinner plates themselves when he caught sight of the prices on the menu, but Gus just smiled. "Happy Birthday, Ryan, a wee bit early. Order anythin' ye like."

"Wow, Gus, I don't know what to say."

"Just say y'er hungry."

Ryan laughed. "Starving. Always."

"Good." Gus eyed the menu and decided immediately what to order.

"Hello, gentlemen. I'm Amanda, and it's my good fortune that I will be taking care of you tonight." She smiled at Ryan but then turned and winked at Gus. His cheeks took on color. Women in Florida were certainly a friendly lot.

"What can I get you to drink?"

"Cola, please, no ice," Ryan said.

"The same," Gus added.

"Really? Nothing from the bar?" she asked.

"Thank ye, no." The moment the words were out of his mouth he cringed; there it was, the look on her face that most women he met got the first time they heard him speak.

"Oh... I heard about you! You're our guest from Scotland visiting by way of Detroit." Again, she winked.

"Aye," Gus replied.

"Marsha told me all about you."

"I'll have to thank her later for makin' sure that I feel welcome wherever I go."

Now color illuminated the waitress's face. "I'll be right back with your drinks and to take your order."

"You are so lucky," Ryan said, as soon as their server was out of earshot.

"How do ye mean?"

"Women fall all over themselves when you're around. Lucky."

Gus knew Ryan well enough to know that there was more to the thought than he was saying. "Why is that so lucky? Is there someone ye wish would be fallin' all over herself where y'er concerned?"

Ryan's cheeks burned; now it was his turn to blush. "Maybe."

"Maybe..." Gus said, the corner of his lip curling up slightly. "Definitely, I'd say. So tell me about her."

"Maybe... later. What about you, Gus? You still hanging out with that girl, Till?"

"I don't know if 'hangin' out' is the proper term. We're friends." As he spoke the words, Gus hoped that they were still actually true. The way things were between them right now... he tried to push the thought from his mind and focus on the lad sitting across from him.

Ryan smirked. "Sure. *Friends.*"

Gus decided it was time to change the subject. "How's yer Ma gettin' on at work?"

"She's working two jobs... one at the diner, and one helping out the lady we rent the apartment from. Taking her on errands, fixing her hair and such. And she's going to school to get her home health aide training, so I don't really see her much right now."

"Ye didn't see her much when ye lived back in Michigan, either, only there was no hope things would be better in the future. At least now, with her trainin' there's an end date, and then she'll be able to get one better job. That will mean you two can see each other a lot more."

"By then I'll be ready to start college," Ryan replied softly, tilting his water glass back and forth until the ice cubes spun in circles. "But you're right. It is still better here than it was back there. Which makes me wonder..." He looked up at Gus now, his stare direct. "Why do you stay?"

Gus answered simply. "My life is there."

"You could move your life. You could bring it down here. The weather is a hell of a lot better."

"Mind yer language..."

"Sorry."

"You two ready to order?" Amanda asked, setting down their drinks and then holding her pen at the ready.

"I'll have the New York strip, medium well, with the mashed potatoes, please," Gus replied.

"Make it two," Ryan added, handing over his menu.

"Very good. I'll be back with some bread," she said, and then she was gone.

Soon after, Gus watched with satisfaction as Ryan devoured every scrap of food on his plate, while he himself only felt up to picking at his steak. He was quite content to hand what he could not eat over to Ryan to let him finish it, and then to let the lad order dessert as well, as Gus nursed a cup of coffee.

"Ugh," Ryan said at last, pushing his last clean plate away. "I'm stuffed. I think I better walk some of this off before I get into a moving vehicle."

"Want to check out the beach?"

"At least check out the *girls* on the beach."

Gus shook his head as he settled the bill and slowly rose from his chair. In the glow of Ryan's youthful exuberance, he suddenly felt very old.

The boy had certainly changed in the short time he'd been living here. He was turning into the better version of himself that Gus always imagined was there, and was pleased that helping them relocate had been the right decision even though it had been difficult for him to give up his role as Ryan's Fairy Godfather.

Once they reached the beach, Ryan shook his head. "Come on, Gus. This is Florida. You HAVE to take off your boots." He slipped out of his well-worn sneakers and set them beside a lounge chair at the edge of the sand. "It's like, a law."

Gus sighed and dropped to one knee, beginning to unlace his boot. "If it'll make ye happy..."

"VERY happy." Ryan laughed.

Gus stuffed his socks into his boots and left them beside Ryan's sneakers. The sand felt cool in the evening air. The sun was just beginning to sink on the horizon, they'd have plenty of time for a walk and a chat before it got dark.

They continued on in silence for a while, Gus stopping every so often to pick up a seashell from the shore to examine it. Of all the shells he found he saved only two, imagining one as a keepsake for himself, and one as something of a peace offering for Till when he got back. He could have bought her a souvenir but he knew her too well; she would much rather have something sentimental that he found himself amidst innumerable grains of sand on a distant shore than a plastic flamingo magnet from the gift shop.

"So how is yer Ma *really* doin'?" Gus asked at last.

"She's happy here," Ryan said. "First time in my life I can remember seeing her happy. She loves the weather, being able to see such beautiful places, even if we can't get to the public beach very often because of her schedule." His gaze drifted along a row of beautiful women lying on towels near the shore, then out to the sea and back finally to Gus. "I can't thank you enough, Gus, for making this possible for us. I'm... I'm happy here."

"I'm glad, Ryan."

"Only...I really wish you'd think about moving here, too."

Gus sighed. "Ryan--"

"Hear me out," Ryan insisted, stopping where they were. There was no one in the immediate area to hear, and he began speaking faster than Gus had ever heard him talk before. "I know that your work is very important to you, and I'm not talking about the bookstore. I'm talking about the work that you and Till do at night. With people like me. How you help them, and keep them from self-destructing, if you can. Or whatever else it is you do with the rest of them, I don't know."

"Ryan..."

"I'm not finished!" Ryan put his hands in the air and continued. "I know, Gus. I know you're not quite human. I know your work is more than just being a mentor for at-risk kids. I know that it's..." He paused finally, slowly whispering the final word. "Magic."

The very last of the color that remained disappeared from Gus's face.

"It's okay, really," Ryan insisted, putting a hand on Gus's shoulder. "You're not the one who let the secret slip. It was my new mentor, Mason. Mason... he's... unique. He's..." Ryan smiled a little. "Okay, he's flamboyant as hell and completely crazy. I like him. But he was very obviously not your average Joe when I met him. It didn't take me long to get the truth out of him. Though to be honest, Gus, the idea of applying the term Fairy Godfather to you still seems absolutely ridiculous."

Gus wasn't laughing, even as Ryan did. Ryan took note and turned serious again.

"I know I wasn't supposed to find out, but it just happened. So now I know, what's the issue? It's not like I've ever asked Mason to use his powers for anything for me, though looking back I think I can see the times when you definitely did. But most of what you did for me you did on your own, just because you're a good man, Gus. Whatever else you may or may not be. You're a good man, and that's why you helped me. Now I wish *I* could help *you*."

Gus's mouth felt dry as he tried to speak. "Why would ye think I need helpin'?"

Ryan gave him a look that said he should know better. "I've known you a long time. I've watched you change. I have seen you reserved, I have seen you focused, and resolved. Now, I've seen you sad— heartbroken, really, if your behavior since you got here tells me anything. And it bothers me. It really isn't right that someone who has done so much to help others should be so down."

Gus didn't know what to say to that, so he said nothing.

"I know that you're sad because of something to do with Till," Ryan continued. "I see the way women go crazy over you, but you don't notice a single one of them. Till is the one you want, but for whatever reason, it hasn't worked out. I don't want to pry. But I just thought if you could move down here and put some distance between the two of you, permanently, it might help. Give you a fresh start."

Gus gave him a look that said there must be more to Ryan's idea than that.

"Yes, I admit, there is a selfish component to this. I'm not ashamed or too cool or whatever to admit that I miss having you around. You're the closest thing I've had to a father figure in my life, ever. So yeah, I wish you were around more."

"There might be a way for me to be around more now, anyway," Gus said, drawing his hand along the scruff on his chin. "The only reason I transferred you over to Mason was because ye were not supposed to find out the truth. Now that ye know…" He shook his head. "There's no reason I can't… use the means at my disposal… to come and visit ye more often."

"Really?" Ryan's eyes lit up. "You can… *do that*?"

"I can do a lot of things…" Gus said, in all seriousness. "But I can't move here, Ryan. Life for me is back in Michigan, workin' with Till. There are other people I have to consider here."

"You always consider everyone before yourself. When is it your turn?"

Gus did not admit that the same question had crossed his mind, during his walk earlier in the day. "Someday, maybe. For now, it's my job to look after others, includin' Till, and that's what I'm goin' to do."

"I understand." Ryan stuck out his hand toward Gus. "I know that… you were supposed to stay the weekend. But I can see how worried you are, about something. About Till, I'm betting. Did you two fight before you came here?" Ryan asked, sounding more grown up than Gus could ever remember.

"It's more complicated than just a fight."

"Look, if you want to change your flight, go back early, or just wave your wand and teleport yourself back, or whatever it is you Fairy Godpeople do, then I'll understand. Sometimes a man's got to do what a man's got to do. And tonight… I have a history paper that I have to do."

Gus nodded his approval. "I'm proud of ye, lad."

Ryan shrugged, looking away. "That's all I ever wanted, really. To make you proud of me."

Gus gave him a strong pat on the back. "Come on, then, we'd best be getting' ye home."

* * *

Not a word was spoken between the two as music blared from the convertible's speakers, all the way back from the hotel until the moment they turned the corner onto the street where Ryan lived.

He quickly reached for the dial to turn down the volume, causing Gus to raise an eyebrow. How different this considerate young man before him was from the rebellious one he'd first met at the youth center, years ago.

"The locals don't appreciate my taste in music," Ryan explained, laughing a little. "But they're nice people. It's a good trade off."

"Wise man," Gus said, watching as Ryan waved to several little old ladies watering their flowerbeds on the perfectly landscaped street.

"We rent the upstairs level from Mrs. Richards," Ryan explained, "She's really nice… but… you know that already, don't you? You are the one who arranged the whole thing."

Now Gus shrugged a little as he pulled the car into the driveway. "Mrs. Richards needed some good in her life, too. So it was a healthy arrangement, for everyone."

"I'm grateful."

"I'm glad y'er happy here."

Gus followed Ryan to the door and extended his hand. "Was good to see ye. Especially to see y'er doin' so well. Now be sure to mind Mason… I know he's different, but y'er his student now… and I'm sure he will teach ye things that never would have occurred to me."

Ryan laughed. "Of that, I am certain." He looked down at the ground as he shook Gus's hand. "Will I… see you from time to time?"

"My word upon it. Only I hate keepin' secrets from yer ma, and she would know that I couldn't afford to fly out here very often on a bookseller's wages."

"I understand."

"There's always email. And… though I hate to do it," Gus cringed, "Video chat."

"You'd consider it?"

"Yeah, I'll consider it."

Ryan threw his arms around Gus and gave him a manly pat on the back before letting him go. "Thanks, Gus. For everything. And for what it's worth…" He paused with his key in the lock, "I hope you can find some peace about Till. Really."

"Thanks, Ryan. I do too."

Chapter Twenty-Two

Stranded

GUS RUSHED BACK TO HIS ROOM the moment he arrived at the hotel. There was no time left to waste, standing on ceremony. He'd wanted to start and finish this trip as a human would, but that wasn't who he was, not entirely. He *was* a Fairy Godfather, and he would do whatever he had to do to get back to Till's side as quickly as possible.

He'd signed up for automatic check out when he'd booked the room, so there was no need to let anyone know he was leaving town early. The rental car people would mysteriously find the car back in their lot first thing Sunday morning, as planned.

Back in his room where no one could see him, he slung his backpack over his shoulder, picked up his suitcase, and closed his eyes.

One word filled his mind as he imagined himself teleporting back: *home.*

He was alarmed to discover when he opened his eyes again that he was still in his hotel room.

"No..." he whispered, concentrating harder. "This can't be happenin'..."

Again, his attempt at teleportation failed. It was the first time his powers had entirely failed him since he'd taken charge of them while at university; and now was the worst possible time it could be happening.

"No, no, no, no..." Gus groaned, flopping down onto the bed and closing his eyes. Something was seriously wrong with him now, as well as with Till. He attempted in this moment to call out to her across the miles, to make a connection with her mind and let her know that he was sorry, that he would be coming home as soon as he could get there and that they'd sort everything out then.

His attempts to reach her were met with complete silence.

"Damn," he whispered, and finally he pulled the cell phone out of his pocket and dialed the airline. "Yes, this is Gus Duncan, I have a reservation for the 7:45 nonstop from Tampa to Detroit on Sunday mornin'. I was wonderin' if there is a flight out that leaves tonight instead? Yes, I know there will be a fee to change my ticket, I don't care about that… I—"

"Hold please," the woman on the other end of the line replied. Gus could hear her typing furiously at a keyboard for several minutes before she spoke again; a torturous eternity to him. "There is a 9:55 nonstop back to Detroit in the morning, that's the best I can offer you."

"I'll take that for now, and try another airline to see if I can get back sooner. It's an emergency." He cursed himself for having been so foolish as to ever leave Till in such a state, no matter what it was doing to him to see her in it.

"You're confirmed on the 9:55 nonstop from Tampa to Detroit. Do you want your reservation number?" she replied at last.

"Please," Gus said, typing the number into the notepad on his phone as she recited it. "Thank ye kindly." He hung up and ran his hands over his face, feeling panicked.

Just to be sure it wasn't a momentary lapse, he tried once again to think himself back home, but it was no use. It was if there was a broken link between him and his powers, and he couldn't help but think that severed connection originated with the break between him and Till. He needed to find out. He needed to find her.

He needed to get home.

He thought about attempting to call her, but decided it was no use. She'd be too angry by this point to pick up.

Too restless to lie down and close his aching eyes, he sought out the shore one last time, to try to get some sense of where he was now and what he was supposed to do next.

He'd originally counted upon having three whole days away to try to talk some sense into himself; to knock the idea back out of his head that kept coming to it, again and again no matter what he did. That idea was that he and Till were meant to be together, not only as partners in their fairy work but in life— as lovers and soul mates.

He didn't get far down the beach before he saw a line of glowing tiki torches lighting the night, and row after row of folding white chairs set up in the sand.

A couple stood at the end of a rope lined aisle; she in a flowing white dress, he in a tuxedo, and Gus was wounded by the sight. The pair was, at this very moment, exchanging wedding vows.

He regretted eating dinner. He managed to gulp the wave of nausea back, though the sensation only seemed amplified now by the rolling waves as they crashed onto the beach.

He needed to sit down.

He paced a respectful distance away from the ceremony in progress and then plunked down, just as he was, onto the sand. He shifted, reaching into his pocket and pulling out the two seashells he'd picked up earlier.

For a moment he considered casting them back into the sea from which they'd come, but instead his hand closed tightly around them. As his eyes slipped shut and he remembered with excruciating clarity the softness of Till's skin against his, the sharp edges of the shells threatened to breach his palm.

"It won't do you any good to keep it all inside," a voice said now, and Gus startled. He was unaccustomed to anyone being able to sneak up on him that way.

"Is stealth approach a class they teach ye in all that post-grad work, ye helpers?" he growled, shoving the shells back into his pocket and staring up at the woman before him.

"Something of the sort," Liz said, dropping down into the sand to sit beside him. "What we gain in one skill set we unfortunately lose in another. I guess they figure it keeps things fair."

"What kind of skills do ye lose?" Gus asked, figuring there was no way to get rid of her right away, he may as well make small talk and hope she tired of it. All the while he focused his energy on just being present in the moment, hoping whatever control he still may have over his powers would allow him to conceal his thoughts of Till from Liz, and his deepest feelings for Till, from Till.

"Well, to tell you the truth we suck at in-depth mind reading."

"Really now?" Gus sat up straighter and looked directly at her. "That would seem to be a major handicap in the performance of yer duties." He questioned how she knew so much about him the second he'd landed in town as she claimed, then, but kept that thought to himself for the moment. Something here didn't add up. For now, he decided he'd just try to keep her talking.

"It is. But it makes us better listeners," Liz explained. "If we could just know it all the moment we set eyes on a fairy in trouble, then we'd get lazy. We'd be tempted to use magic to try to solve everything. But since their problems are usually created by magic or the laws that govern it, we'd only manage to confuse the situation." She tugged at the hem of her mini-dress and then crossed her long, tan legs. Her platinum hair blew astray in the breeze and she brushed it back with a graceful gesture. "Of course, it doesn't take a mind reader to know that the sight of that wedding over there made you feel physically ill. You turned absolutely green, and you've stayed that way."

Gus raked his hand through the sand. "No comment."

"That only reinforces my theory," Liz replied, mirroring his motion and tracing her long, slender fingers through the beach's snow white surface. "It's a woman that has you so distraught. And from the way I've seen you completely disregard every human woman you've seen since you set foot here, I'm guessing the one that has you so brokenhearted has more *exotic* DNA."

"Listen, Liz, I know y'er only tryin' to help, but this is not helpin'. So I'd rather ye just left me on my own."

"Going to be a long weekend if you keep at this," Liz warned. "Maybe you just need something to put you in more of a mood to talk." She waved her hand and a picnic basket appeared before her. She held it up and pulled back the blanket that covered its contents. "Pick your poison, Gus Duncan. There's a box of chocolate mint truffles, a thermos of chocolate milk, a dozen chocolate chip cookies, and a flask of pure syrup. Your choice."

"No thanks."

"Oh come on…" She reached into the basket and pulled out a truffle. "I've had a hell of a week on the day job, I know that I'm certainly ready to relax."

"Suit yerself. I can't afford to get foggy in the least, I have a flight to catch in the mornin'." Immediately he hated himself for letting that piece of information slip. She looked more than a little alarmed and glanced at him sideways.

"Going home early? Do you think that's wise? After all you did come here to get some space; that much is clear. Even if you did use the excuse of visiting your little local friend, I can tell that you needed the trip here more than he needed to see you."

"Shows how much you know," Gus retorted. "He asked me to move here. Turns out he misses me as a mentor more than I realized."

"So move here! You can certainly figure out a way to keep your charges if you want to, you're a darling around DCTU. They open doors for you that for others remain securely locked."

"Now how would ye know such a thing? Has someone been tellin' tales?" Gus grew increasingly suspicious of this woman, and hoped to flush out the truth in a hurry so he could move on his way.

"I've heard your name around campus... more than once. I happen to know a few people who work with the board of governors..." Now she was the one who clearly regretted saying what she'd been thinking.

"I knew it. Would one of those 'friends on the board' happen to be a blond guy, about my height, with a bad attitude and more power than should be afforded anyone with an ego so huge?"

"Gus..." Liz pulled the flask out of the basket now, yanked the cap off and took a long slug of pure chocolate syrup. She tried to hand it to him, and in that moment, another voice was heard just behind them.

"Gus?"

Gus froze. How could this be happening? "Till?" He managed to finally rise to his feet and turned to see Till standing before him with tears in her eyes.

"So, you're on vacation. Having a good time too, from the looks of it." Till's voice shook with emotion, though Gus couldn't tell in this moment if it was anguish or rage.

"Till, let me explain—"

"You don't have to explain to me! You don't owe me anything." Tears streamed down her face and she turned on her heel. Gus followed as Till increased her pace, kicking up sand behind her. "I go through all of this... drive myself near crazy... protecting you, doing everything I can to keep things the way they're supposed to be, and for what? I find you in Florida on a beach, drinking with some barmaid!"

"Till, she's one of us! She's a helper, and she thought she—"

"Could *help* you? Oh, I bet she could think of a hundred different ways she'd *love* to try. I thought they were all against the rules."

Gus grasped hold of her arm and tried to turn her toward him. "Till, please, listen. I tried to get home earlier tonight, I tried to reach you. That's got to be how you found me. But I couldn't teleport, Till. Somethin's gone wrong, I can't—"

"No, *you* listen," Till whispered through gritted teeth. "Just… forget I was ever here. Please. I'm… I'm going home."

"Wait!" he begged, "Take me back with you, Tilda Mae, please. My powers have failed, I can't get back before morning otherwise. Take me back with you now, we can talk about everything, figure it all out together. I know we must have somethin' we need talkin' about, otherwise—"

"Otherwise I wouldn't be keeping you out of my thoughts? Otherwise you wouldn't be doing your best to keep me out of yours?" Her shoulders shook as she wept. "Maybe we shouldn't be partners anymore."

"Don't say that, please! Take me back with you now. I promise, we'll—"

"Get yourself back. If it means that much to you, you must be able to do it."

"Till, I already told you, something has happened to me and I can't—"

"Right. Can't." Till wiped at her face furiously to try to banish the tears as they fell. "If that tart over there with the fake bake and bottle blonde hair means nothing to you then come back now. Right now. Then we can talk."

"Till, I need your help to get back," Gus repeated, but she just wouldn't hear him. He pulled the shells out of his pocket and held out the one he'd picked up for her toward her. "Do you think anyone else could ever catch my eye?"

Till looked away, grasping hold of the shell and staring at it, avoiding Gus's gaze.

"Listen to me carefully now," he whispered, leaning closer. "There's more goin' on here with this fairy helper than is right. Someone put her up to tryin' to befriend me and I'm bettin' I know just who. I have to find out. If it's who I think it is…"

"I'm not listening to any more of this." Till threw the shell at him and Gus snatched it out of the air. "You've made it clear what your priorities are. Now I have to reexamine mine."

"Tilda Mae!"

She shook her head, folded her arms over her chest, and then disappeared.

Gus stared down at the spot where she'd been standing; at her footprints still in the sand, and wished so much he could have taken her into his arms that moment and told her exactly what his only priority was.

He jammed the seashells back into his pocket and returned to where Liz was waiting, still taking sips from the silver flask and looking very much 'relaxed' by this point.

"Now is time for ye to do the listenin'," Gus roared, taking the flask away from her and throwing it out into the surf. "What did he offer ye? Or what does he have on ye, that ye'd be willin' to try to cause another Fairy Godparent's downfall just to pay the debt?"

"Gus…" Liz rose on unsteady feet and threw her arms around one of his. "You don't know how powerful he is, how far his reach goes…"

"So it is Lane, then? Put ye up to pretendin' that ye knew who I was when I walked into the bar, all of it?"

"All of it." Liz gulped hard. "I told you, helpers can't read. We can listen and go by body language and all of that, we become keen observers of fairy nature. But I couldn't read you when you walked into that bar any more than I can read you now. Only now I don't have to. Lane was right, there is something more than just partnership going on with you and Till, and it's a danger— to you, to her, to *everyone*."

"Stay out of it, Liz. Ye've done all the *helpin'* I intend to allow." Gus turned and started to walk away. He paused. "Unless…"

She shifted nervously. "Unless?"

"Ye really do want to help me. You've obviously figured out by this point that I'm having difficulties right now, or I'd have transported myself right after Till. You want to help me? Then send me home."

Her eyes widened with terror. "I… I can't. Gus. Even if I wanted to, which I'm not sure I do, I can't. If Lane found out—"

"What have you to fear from Lane, anyway?"

"We ALL have PLENTY to fear from Lane!" she shouted at last. "Haven't you figured it out yet? He's running the board by default. They're old, and weak, and they can't stand up to him any better than I could. He's powerful, Gus, and he's made up his mind about you. He has his sights set on you and anyone who helps you, *really* helps you, will suffer the consequences. I can't get involved. I'm sorry."

"Sorry. Right. Well if y'er not goin' to help, then get the hell out of my way."

She grasped hold of his hand, tugging him backward once more. "Gus, be careful with Lane, please. He really has it in for you and Till. He's not going to stop until he ruins whatever it is that you have left. And he doesn't give a damn who else he has to hurt in the process."

"He can try what he wants on me," Gus called back over his shoulder after finally breaking free. "But if he so much as touches a hair on Till's head, he will regret the day he was born."

* * *

Gus was weak and trembling as he returned to his room and prepared to try again to do exactly what he'd failed at before— transport himself back home without the use of an airplane.

He attempted to concentrate on where he wanted to go, but Till's anguish kept invading his thoughts. He experienced that moment when she saw him with Liz as physically painful, just as she had. He still ached, inside and all over, and he had to accept that something was seriously wrong as he failed not once, not twice, but half a dozen times more to transport himself as far as across the hotel room.

Each attempt left him weaker, until his knees finally gave out beneath him and he dropped to the floor. Sickened and out of breath, he fought the raging storm in his stomach. This inability to control his powers was unbelievable. He cursed himself again for taking this ill-advised trip to begin with. He'd wanted to run, but he'd neglected to remember the lesson he'd already learned earlier in life; there is no distance far enough to travel to be successful in outrunning yourself.

He fought to catch his breath and finally, struggled to his feet. As soon as his head felt clear enough he gathered up his bags and drove to the airport as fast as he could.

He went from airline counter to airline counter until he found the first flight out: one with a standby seat available that made a connection in Atlanta on the way back to Detroit. He begged the woman behind the counter to give him that single seat. Finally she could resist his pleading no longer, and Gus held a boarding pass for the flight in his trembling hands.

He sank to the floor with his back up against the wall at the packed gate and waited to board his flight. He closed his eyes, considering how all this could have happened.

The only thing he could figure was that keeping Till out of his thoughts for so long, when she had clearly been trying so hard to get into them, had drained every last ounce of strength from his soul.

He knew that, as much as he was weakened from being at odds with Till, the human part of his DNA was going to win this time.

For the first time in his life, he loathed the human in him that remained.

It seemed unthinkably cruel that his powers had failed him so when he had never needed them more.

Counting down the seconds until he could finally get back into the air and pointed in the right direction, Gus watched the palm trees outside sway in the restless breeze, and contemplated just how far he really was from home.

Chapter Twenty-Three

Chaos

THE MOMENT HIS FEET HIT THE FAMILIAR GRAVEL on the driveway of the house on Finch Street, Gus searched frantically for something of Till to grab on to.

The physical sense of her presence he could only describe as a warmth he'd never known before. A trail of her thoughts. Anything that would allow him to find her.

He knew that he had to try, somehow, to get her to listen. He wondered how he'd begin to explain what was in his heart to her, since he could hardly explain it to himself.

The panic within Gus was unlike anything he had ever experienced.

The look he'd last seen in Till's eyes, accompanied by heartache she could not conceal, had been overwhelming enough to shatter him. The moment her gaze had met his, it was as though a sound so primal, so visceral pierced his psyche that it caused him physical agony, just as she experienced it.

In her heart, and in his head, she was wailing.

He'd never seen her that way, and the experience pulled the air from his lungs and stole the cadence of his heart. To think that he could be the cause of so much suffering for her was more than merely unfathomable; it was unbearable.

Whatever he had to do to make things right, he would find a way. He would make them, at the very least, as right as he possibly could.

"Tilda Mae!" he cried, bursting through the front door of the house. "Tilda Mae please, are ye here? I need to talk to ye. I need to tell ye everythin'. I… I think I know what's wrong, with both of us."

His frantic pace increased as he searched room after empty room. Till was nowhere to be seen, and he couldn't begin to get a fix on where she might have gone. "God, Tilda Mae, if ever I needed something of ye to keep close to me... a sign, a way to somehow find my way back to ye..." he whispered into the silence, as he stood at the door to her bedroom and stopped just as he was about to go in.

He didn't know what else to do at this point, and so, steeling himself for the emotions he knew lay in wait for him just beyond the barrier, he thrust open the door, and strode inside.

The room was a disaster, as were the rooms he'd passed to get here. Chaos reigned in the house, as if Till had been frantically searching for something but unable to find it.

His steps slowed as he moved toward her bed. He grasped hold of her pillow and buried his face in it, taking in the faint fragrance of her perfume.

The memories of the hours he had spent in that bed, on that one perfect night, threatened to destroy what little remained of his sanity. Yet those memories were also, he believed, the very thing that might save them both in the end.

He focused on them as closely as he could, trying to recall the feeling of her body beside his, reaching out with his mind and heart to wherever she may be, to call her back to him, to his arms. To guide her back to a place where they could figure this all out together.

A flash of a vision entered his mind. It lasted only a split second, too quick for Gus to latch onto it or make any sense of it. Still, something was happening here... he began to feel stronger, just being in her room, near her things.

At last he released the pillow and moved toward her closet. Inside, he saw the dress she'd worn the night his One Wish was granted; the one he had so slowly removed and found the silken slip beneath before finally reaching her soft, ivory skin.

Another flash crossed his mind; this time he saw her wandering; as if she was unsure where she was supposed to go. "I want to find ye, Tilda Mae," he whispered. "*Please*, help me find ye."

He turned from the closet, and there, on the vanity beside the bed, he found something so devastating he could hardly comprehend it. It was the necklace he'd given her for Christmas: the key to his heart.

For the first time he knew of since she'd received the gift, she had taken it off.

He picked it up and clasped it in his palm. "No. Please, Till, don't give up on me yet."

The moment the metal made contact with his skin, another flash of clairvoyance, this one long enough to actually make sense of, rushed through his mind.

"Please let this be the key to bringin' ye back home," he whispered, as he gently undid the clasp and actually put the necklace on. It fell against his chest and immediately, the vision of her intensified. Whether it was because she had worn it so close to her heart for so long that it had actually become a part of her in some way, Gus didn't know. He was only grateful for whatever power it now seemed, on its own, to possess.

"I'm comin' to find ye, Till. My word upon it." He once again brushed his hand over her pillow and concentrated on the resurgence of power he felt stirring inside of him. In an instant, his ability to transport returned to him. In that moment, he was more determined to find her than he had ever been to accomplish anything in his life.

* * *

Gus's initial hopes of tracking her down were quickly dashed, as he spent a long and anxious night trying, continually, to get a fix on Till's thoughts and thereby, her location.

There was nothing for him to find, and he couldn't believe that she had been able to keep the barriers between them up so long, without so much as wavering for a moment. She could have used distance as an aid; the farther apart two Fairy Godparents were, the harder it was to read their thoughts, even for those who knew them best.

Still, there was a time long ago when she'd been able to read his thoughts all the way from Scotland to locate him. With a bond that strong it should work both ways; he should have, at this point, some general idea of where she'd gone.

He had an eerie, terrifying sense that she'd been wandering from place to place, and so he did his best to follow the faintest trail that he could find. It led him in circles around the globe, as he visited not only all the stops that they'd made during their hide and seek game, but also anywhere else that might be close to her heart— somewhere she might go when she was afraid or felt she was in trouble.

He even visited her attic bedroom at her parents' house, thinking she might revert to going back to her childhood home in her distress. Finding it empty, he decided then to finally break down and ask if her family had seen her.

He teleported from the room and onto the front porch. He knocked on the door, hands trembling as he waited. It was too early yet for Mr. and Mrs. Nesbitt to have left for the shop, they'd still be having their breakfast now.

"Gus!" Clara Nesbitt said, waving for him to come in out of the unseasonal morning chill. "Have you seen Till this morning? I was awfully worried about her last night when I spoke to her."

"Ye spoke to Till last night?"

"I called her to ask if she could come in a little late, cover a split shift because Amber had something she had to do today. She said she wouldn't be coming in at all, that she didn't feel well. I told her that with as often as that's been happening it was time to see a doctor and, well, she just sort of freaked out on me."

"What do ye mean, 'freaked out'?"

"She stopped making sense."

"Missus, it's very important that ye tell me everythin' you remember her sayin'. To the word. Very important."

"She said something about how she didn't want to be who she was any more. That she was tired of working all the time and not having a life. She said she just wanted to be normal, that she just wanted to be happy..." She averted her gaze. "Your name came up a time or two, Gus, I have to admit. But it didn't make sense what she said."

"Please, ye have to tell me exactly what she said."

"It's difficult for me to remember, she was talking so fast," Mrs. Nesbitt continued. "Something about you telling her she was forgetting things when she wasn't. But the same thing has been happening with me. I've seen her memory lapse several times lately, during the simplest tasks at work. She's been so distracted, there is only one explanation I can possibly come up with."

Gus was afraid of what she was going to say next, and steadied himself.

"In case you haven't noticed, Gus, I believe my daughter is in love with you."

Gus sighed slowly, and, looking her directly in the eyes, he spoke his heart. "The feelin' is mutual."

"Then talk to her, Gus, please." Mrs. Nesbitt took hold of Gus's shaking hands. "I don't know what it is that you two have argued about, but it's obviously really upset her. Go to her. Fix whatever it is between the two of you is broken. For both your sakes."

"Am goin' to try, Missus, I promise ye. Thanks." He hurried around the corner, out of sight, and in that moment he had a flash of a sliver of a thought go through his mind: Till, back at the house on Finch Street.

"Right…" Gus suddenly felt even more energized. It was as though admitting his feelings to someone — anyone — instead of fighting them had increased his flagging powers tenfold. He'd waste no time in getting back to the house. Till's time was running out, he knew it— the longer she was beyond his ability to sense, the more he feared for her safety.

"Tilda Mae!" he called again as he unlocked the door with a thought and rushed into the kitchen. He observed once more that the house was a mess. There were books and papers strewn all over the usually spotless kitchen table and across the floor leading into the bedroom. Instead of allowing himself to be pulled back into the past by his memories again now, he focused on trying to find any clues that could help to save his future.

He noticed a journal of some kind with several bookmarks sticking out of the top; obviously notes were flagged that Till wanted to refer back to quickly. Willing to leave no stone unturned, he silently begged her forgiveness and tore into the pages, reading as quickly as he could. Nothing that was scribbled within made any sense to him at all, and that worried him all the more.

He realized there was one other person in the world that may have some clue where she was… and though he hated the thought of seeking out that man to ask, in the end he found he didn't have to.

The moment he made his way back to the front door and closed it behind him, he discovered Lane waiting for him on the porch, arms crossed as he leaned against the wall. He had a self-righteous expression on his face that turned Gus's stomach and made his blood pulse faster through his veins.

"Son of a bitch," Gus spat, advancing on Lane to the point where Lane held his hands up to keep Gus from grabbing hold of him. "What have ye done to her?"

"Done to her? I haven't even seen her," Lane answered, eerily serene. "Question is, what have *you* done to her, Gus?"

It was the first time in years that Lane had addressed him by his proper name, and it made Gus shudder. "What are ye after here, Lane?"

"Same thing you are, I'm looking for Till. Trying to help her."

"She doesn't need yer help."

"You so sure of that?" He licked his lips, savoring the words he had next to say. "Why are you so afraid of me?"

"Afraid *for* her. Not *of* you."

So why can't you find her, Leprechaun?

Gus ignored Lane's taunt and tried to think things through. "Her family hasn't seen her, either..."

"Honest truth here," Lane said, though Gus wasn't sure he believed anything that came out of the man's mouth. "I don't know what it is, but I just can't get a read on her. She must have retreated completely within her own thoughts to be able to keep us both out."

"Why would you say that?" Gus crossed his arms defensively, beginning to pace. There was no hiding now just how terrified he was that something horrible was happening to her.

"Come on, Gus, everyone can tell how you feel. Well, except maybe Till. It's obvious to everyone else that you know her *better than anyone*."

Gus resisted the urge to rearrange the features on Lane's smug little face. He had bigger problems. He still had to find Till.

"Word has it the last one to see her was you," Lane continued, casually buffing his nails on his shirt. "I'm more than happy to offer my assistance to you. Perhaps together we can—"

"No thanks," Gus replied, heading for the door. "We're all better off without yer kind of 'help'."

"Suit yourself," Lane said, feigning regret. "I just hope someone can find her, before she completely shuts down."

* * *

Fueled by a brighter fire and desperation within him, Gus's search began again. He backtracked everywhere he could possibly imagine she might go, and tried several new places just because she said that she had always wanted to see them. Just before he'd transport every time, he'd take hold of the pendant of Till's necklace in his hand, and somehow, it gave him the strength he needed to keep searching.

From Grand Central Terminal in New York to Flinders Street Station in Melbourne, he looked from place to place around the globe, exhausting himself as well as the list of sites he could come up with where she might be hiding.

Then a thought occurred to him that he couldn't believe he hadn't considered sooner. What if she'd gone somewhere and forgotten again about her powers? She could be lost… wandering. Afraid.

He most hated the thought of her ever being afraid.

I promised myself I'd always watch over you, he thought. *How the hell did I ever let it come to this? Where are you?*

Images flooded his consciousness again from the night his One Wish was fulfilled. The feel of her skin beneath his fingertips; the sound of her sigh as he lovingly pressed his lips to her neck. The taste of her kiss, the silk of the slip beneath her dress. Every sense was heightened with the memory of her voice and her words; the way she'd pledged her love to him again and again even though she didn't need to, really— her actions declared them clearly enough.

He believed now that he could actually die if he never felt those sensations again. He had never truly believed that the memories of a One Wish could be so strong, maintain every single detail in total without losing a bit of their intensity, over time. But they were, and they did.

Her love was the most powerful form of magic he had ever known.

When he'd exhausted all corners of the human world he could think to search, his heart led him onward, one place more. To the place that posed the greatest danger to her of all if she did not remember who, and what, she was.

Chapter Twenty-Four
Found and Lost

WHEN GUS FINALLY DID FIND TILL, she was pacing back and forth behind the Music building on the campus of Dreams Come True University, looking like she had never seen the place before in her life.

She looked as terrified as he felt. He felt as desperate as she did, with her feelings flooding toward him and submerging them both the moment she laid eyes on him.

She ran up to him, her voice tremulous as she called to him. "Gus! I'm so glad to see you. I don't know how I wandered so far from home, but I got lost. Last thing I remember I was outside the bookstore and then I was in this place," she trembled as she put her hands upon his shoulders. "Gus, what *is* this place?"

"Till... God, Till," Gus struggled to speak, beyond panic. "It's the Music buildin'. Over there's the library." No recognition registered on her features or in her thoughts. His heart sank. "Don't ye remember? Ye've..." His voice faded as she shook her head. "Spent a lot of time here."

"I'm so afraid," she whispered, grasping him fiercely until he felt the only thing he could possibly do to help her was to pull her closer. It would nearly kill him to hold her in his arms with the knowledge that was all he could do, but she needed him and he wouldn't back away.

"It's gonna be all right, Tilda Mae, I promise ye."

Her eyes glazed over and she stared past him, looking through him. "Tilda Mae... you've called me that before."

Gus couldn't believe what he was hearing. Could her memory failure be that complete? "I've called ye that many times."

"No... I mean you called me that *here*." Till clasped him tighter and tilted her face up to his. Her lips were mere inches from his now, and Gus felt that same familiar tremor as it rose from his knees and enveloped him. His heart pounded mercilessly. What was she talking about? Had something happened here that he had no knowledge of? He remembered that they'd been talking somewhere near here before he confessed his One Wish to her, and she took him back home to fulfill it…

"I remember…" Till first shook her head and then nodded it up and down. Her body continued to tremble as she attempted to sift through her confusion. "You kissed me here for the first time."

"No, that can't be." He had no memory of kissing her here, only back at the house. In fact, he didn't remember much from right before his wish was granted… what had happened?

"You kissed me, and I…" Till took hold of the front of his shirt and kissed him fiercely. Gus fought to resist but his hands found her back and slid down around her waist, holding on for all he was worth. He was beyond his breaking point, completely unable to deny her, whether condemned for it later or not.

Her kiss was as familiar as it was devastating, as wanted as it was feared, as necessary as oxygen. In her kiss he was whole again: in her embrace, he was home.

Till wept as they finally parted.

"We kissed here, and you asked me. You asked me even though you said I wouldn't remember. I shouldn't remember, but I do. I *remember*. We were at the house, and we…" Her words trailed off. She suddenly went weak in the knees, a marionette cut loose from its strings.

She leaned her full weight against him, and Gus held tight to keep her from falling.

"Till, no…" he gasped. "It can't be true."

He swept her up into his arms. He lay her gently down upon the ground, resting her head upon his knee before taking his own head into his hands.

Till was mumbling, barely above a whisper. "I would marry you today," she said, and Gus thought his heart may stop still as stone in his chest. "I love you, Gus, so much. I will always love you."

His breathing grew shallow and he felt as if he might lose consciousness. The world around him spun, faster and tighter, with the speed and shock of her confession. "No. Ye *can't* remember, Till, y'er not meant to remember. What will happen to ye if ye…" All of her behavior finally made sense to him with the missing piece in place. "God, no. Ye've *always remembered*."

"Gus…" She lifted a hand up towards him, brushing it against his cheek. He couldn't stand the earnestness with which she added, "Please…" and he had no choice but to gently gather her into his arms once more.

She tried to kiss him but he turned his head away, still reeling and unsure in the moment what he should do now to keep her as safe as he could.

"Please…" she cried, shivering in his arms. "I've missed you *so much*."

"The rules, Till, don't ye remember? I can't. We can't."

"Rules? I don't understand. What are you talking about?"

"The code…" His eyes widened. Just how selective was her memory now?

"I don't know what you mean," Till insisted, holding on to him for dear life. "Kiss me, Gus, please. I don't want to argue anymore. I don't even know what we were arguing *about*."

Gus's insides twisted and turned in knots as he forced himself to ask her the next thing that came to his mind. "Till, where did we meet?"

"At home, of course. Aunt Tilda introduced us."

He felt some small relief. Even if she had the details wrong, at least she remembered Aunt Tilda.

"But I really fell in love with you at the bookstore," Till added. "That's where we spent the most time together, after you came to work there."

Again, alarms rang in Gus's mind. "But what about this place?"

Till's eyes finally moved from his face and scanned her surroundings. They filled again with confusion. "Where are we, Gus?" She shook so violently her words were barely intelligible now. "I don't understand. Why won't you kiss me? What did I do wrong?"

"Nothin', darlin', absolutely nothin'." He pressed his lips to the top of her head. "We'll figure it out, I promise ye."

"Gus," Till whispered again, resting her head against his shoulder. "I'm so tired. Will you stay with me? While I sleep?"

"Sleep!" He tried to shake her back from the brink of unconsciousness. "No, Till, ye can't sleep. Stay with me. Ye have to stay with me." His past vision of her in an unknown location, sleeping, came back upon him full force. Was this the moment that he had foreseen, and most feared?

"Hold me…" she pleaded, as her eyes slipped shut.

Gus clutched her to his heart, buried his face in her hair, and wept.

Till was dying, he knew it, and there was only one thing that was going to stop her mind from destroying her now.

They were going to have to break the rules, just as his parents had.

He began to wonder if this was why his father had done what he did, marrying his mother.

His shoulders shook with sobs. "If only I could ask… what am I supposed to do? Let her die, and my heart and soul die with her?"

The answer was clear, unquestionable in his mind.

Something inside Gus raged at him for hesitating for even an instant. He knew in that moment exactly what he must do. He placed his hands tenderly upon her face, tilted it toward him, and passionately kissed her.

After a moment that seemed forever, she stirred and smiled up at him.

"Gus, I was dreaming…" she whispered. "Dreaming of you. We were…" Her voice faded and her eyes slipped closed again.

He shook her gently. "Till, y'er not supposed to be dreamin', my darlin'. Y'er supposed to live, and live ye shall, however long we're blessed with. Human and fairy words both be damned, we *will* be together."

He pressed his mouth to hers again, lingering there, and she began to truly awaken. His kiss breathed life back into her, and when they parted, Till's eyes snapped open.

"Gus… what on earth… what are you doing here? What are *we* doing here?"

"You don't remember what we were just…" Gus released Till from his grasp, stood up abruptly, and paced back and forth before her. Till wrung her hands. "What have I done, good God what have I done?" Gus murmured, further confusing her.

"What are you going on about? You haven't done anything…"

Gus dropped to one knee beside her and took hold of her hands. "Till, I need ye to listen to me very carefully. Do ye trust me?"

"Of course," she scoffed, as if the question were ridiculous. "You're my partner, I trust you implicitly."

Gus's hopes soared. "Partner in what?"

"Fairy Godparenting of course!" Till exclaimed, folding her arms over her chest. "What the hell is wrong with you? And what are we doing behind the Music building?"

"It's not just what's wrong with me, Tilda Mae. Somethin' has been wrong between us for a long time, and we're goin' have to fix it so we'll both be saved from this madness."

"You're not making sense."

"Neither were ye, two minutes ago," he rose and resumed his pacing. "Or maybe ye were makin' perfect sense and it's the whole universe that's gone wrong." He took hold of her hands again. "I have to ask ye once more, Tilda Mae, do ye trust me?"

Till's expression was solemn as she squeezed his fingers with her own. "With my life."

"Then trust me now," he begged, pulling her up off of the ground but not letting go of her hand. "We have to get ye someplace safe, and we need help."

"So sleepy," she whispered, suddenly wilting right before his eyes.

"No, ye must NOT go to sleep." He kissed her quickly, and her flagging strength rallied again. He knew it was time to make his heart known— if a declaration of love could do anything to help her, then he would do all he could do to help her.

"Tilda Mae, I am madly in love with ye. I always have been, always will be. I want to be the one yer deepest secrets are safe with, with nothin' to stand between us anymore. So I'm askin' ye again what I asked ye once before." He knew that she was weak, but trusted that if she would hear and understand anything clearly, that it would be this question. She gazed into his eyes, and he hoped she'd give the same answer she had before. "Will ye marry me, Till?"

"Today, Gus," she whispered without hesitation, caressing his cheek with the back of her hand. "I'd marry you *today*."

"Just hang on, darlin'. We're going to make this right, I promise you." His eyes held no more tears; his focus as clear as his emotions. "We've got to go see a man about a weddin'."

Chapter Twenty-Five

Sanctuary

IT WAS ALWAYS NIGHT ON THE CAMPUS of DCTU, but it was also currently what residents referred to as "rest rotation". Even though no one actually slept, it was a time for calm and quiet, and everything around them was still.

Till was too weak to stand or move, so Gus carried her tenderly in his arms.

"I need ye to listen to me," he whispered, unsure she could hear him. "I need ye to think… of Hannah. We have to find her."

Gus also focused all of his thoughts on Hannah, and weak though she was, he felt Till's powers increasing his own. It didn't take long for him to get a visual snapshot of exactly where they needed to go. He immediately transported them there.

The dormitory was a small, nondescript building hidden behind several others, and looked quite out of place on a campus so grand.

"Hannah!" Gus cried, shattering the silence.

"SHUT UP!" an irate voice called, and Gus had to duck out of the way of a shoe as it came flying out from a third floor window.

"Hannah!" Gus shouted again, and finally, a window on the second story slid open.

"WHAT?" Hannah whispered loudly, making the "shush" motion with her finger over her lips. She was surprised to see Gus, of course, but even more surprised to see that Till seemed to be unconscious in his arms.

"I need y'er help," Gus begged. "Please, let us in."

"I can't! Even if I wanted to, my powers have been capped." Hannah whispered again, and then she sent a thought to Gus. Weak as it was, it took him a moment to translate it: *I am on the thinnest of ice here, I can't take any chances.*

Gus sent back a thought of his own. *All the times ye came to me for help, I never turned ye away. How many times have I asked ye for anythin'?*

She sighed, and he sensed her fear she was going to regret this even as she motioned for him to come closer. *If I show you where the hidden door is, do you think you can open it?*

Gus was certain that he could.

Suddenly some of the bricks in the façade of the building began glowing. Gus focused on them, and the next thing he knew, he and Till were inside.

Hannah stood before them in a fluffy pink robe, over silk pajamas and high-heeled slippers trimmed in feathers.

"This way," she instructed, and Gus followed her up the stairway, which no one ever used because they all just thought themselves where they wanted to go.

They arrived at her tiny dorm room and Hannah shut the door. "What do you want?"

"I need ye to keep an eye on Till for me, just for a little while. She's... not well."

"I can see that. Into the cocoa again?"

"This is deadly serious," Gus insisted, checking the window once more to make sure the commotion hadn't stirred up too much curiosity among the dorm's other residents. "I have to speak to Professor Herrmann right away."

"In the middle of rest rotation? He'll eat you alive."

"He's gonna eat me alive anyway, when he finds out what's goin' on," Gus replied, as he gently lay Till down on Hannah's bed. He paused only a second to whisper into Till's ear and then placed a gentle kiss upon her lips.

"Heyyyyy..." Hannah objected.

Gus glared. "No time for yer attitude, mind? Now, I'm tellin' ye that I need ye to watch over her until I come back. Do not, I repeat, do *not* let her leave."

"How am I supposed to stop her if she decides she really wants to go?" Hannah gestured toward her leg, which bore a stunning, if cumbersome, metal anklet. "It contains traces of iron," she explained. "I'm under house arrest. If she tries to leave, I can't follow to stop her."

Gus looked down at her ankle and then, as much as it pained him to do it, he thought up an identical tether and affixed it to Till's. "There. Now she can't go back without me unlockin' it."

"You *are* serious," Hannah said, twirling a strand of hair around her finger. "What do you want old Herrmann for, anyway?"

"I need him to perform a bondin' ceremony," Gus explained, bolting for the door. "Remember, don't let her out of yer sight. She's not thinkin' straight, and I couldn't bear to lose her now."

"Yeah, sure, fine…" Hannah said, picking up a fashion magazine and beginning to thumb through it. Gus's words echoed in her head, and as he ran from the building and out into the night, he felt her thought cross his mind.

Bonding ceremony!

* * *

Gus was trying to conserve his powers as much as he could, believing he would need them all, and then some, soon enough.

He ran across campus, to the small grouping of simple cottages positioned at the far end of the university. Few professors lived on the grounds of DCTU, and those who did lived an ascetic existence, focused solely on the well-being and training of those under their tutelage.

One of those teachers happened to be the very man Gus sought, however, and he quickly found that Professor Herrmann did not appear as surprised to see him as Gus expected.

Gus had yet to knock on the door when it opened up before him, and the man gestured for him to step in.

"So soon," Professor Herrmann said, with a shake of his head. "That certainly didn't take long."

"What didn't take long?"

"For the two of you to get in over your heads."

Gus blushed, deeply. He was not ashamed of how he felt for Till, though. Her health and happiness were the most important thing to him. The man before him could berate him, insult him, do anything he wanted to him, just so long as he would still help her.

"Ye agreed to our pairing as partners." Gus's anger rose, and he tried his best to contain it. "I take it ye knew this would happen to her?"

"I had no idea what would happen to her, or to you, for that matter," Herrmann said, as he dropped down into a large leather chair and pushed his glasses back up over the bridge of his slim, turned-up nose. "I just knew *something* would."

"Aye, somethin' would," Gus growled. "Well ye were right, sir, somethin' has surely happened to Till, and I believe there is only one way to save her."

"You intend to repeat the same mistake your parents made." Professor Herrmann read Gus's thoughts clearly, as Gus's hands balled into fists at his side.

"I'm tryin' to do better than they did! I don't believe, at this point in our history, that the powers that be can afford to penalize and banish every fairy that falls in love and can't forget it. There aren't enough of us left, and those who are left are all gettin' weaker by the year. Besides..." Gus started, but stopped. He was about to try to explain the feelings he'd had ever since he and Till had kissed again after all that time apart; but he was sure that the professor would just think him delusional or, at least, only madly in love.

"Go on," Herrmann prompted. "Say it."

"Ye'll think me mad," Gus said at last.

Herrmann ran a hand through the remaining hair at his forehead. "Are you mad, Angus Duncan?"

"I am as sane as I have ever been."

"Is she?"

Gus's shoulders slumped. "She's not so much mad as forgetful. And she keeps... fallin' asleep."

"Asleep!" Professor Herrmann jumped out of his chair and grabbed Gus by the jacket. "Why didn't I know this? I should have known this!"

"Ye can't read her now, while I can read her clearer and clearer by the second unless she's unconscious," Gus replied, appearing to be in considerable physical pain from the experience. Herrmann finally let go of him and turned away. "Ye see, I have a theory, Professor Herrmann. My theory is that Till and I are part of a new breed. The next step in the evolution of Fairy Godparents. That we've already bonded... and that nothin' short of death is goin' to break that bond or stop its power. If one of us tries to fight it, deny it, bury the memories so deep that nothin' and no one can reach them..." Gus looked down at the floor. "*Then* it'll destroy us. I think that's what has happened to my Till. My One Wish... she never forgot fulfillin' it. And since that time, our powers haven't grown weaker unless we've fought the truth. When we work together, they only grow *stronger*."

Professor Herrmann paled as he listened. He brought his hand to his chin, deep in thought as Gus went on.

"I think *that's* the big secret," Gus whispered. "That is the piece of the puzzle that Till never truly understood. She thought that the next generation would at least be as strong as their parents. That fraternization would prevent the powers gettin' any weaker in any children produced by the union. But the truth is, if the right couple is joined, sealed with a wish and they bond to each other's souls, their own abilities *only increase over time*."

Professor Herrmann said nothing, just took his head into his hands and stood motionless. His change in posture told Gus that not only was he on to something, his theory was entirely correct.

"As they grow closer, they become ever more powerful, and *that* is the reason fairies are not allowed to fraternize. For many pairs, it would probably turn out to be nothin' but a big mess if they remembered, because they were never meant to be together over time. But for that rare, precious few... for Till and I..." His voice faded, and he cleared his throat before continuing. "We could be *so much more* than we already are, and that fact scares *the livin' hell* out of people like yerself, and Lane, and the bloody board that nearly denied Till and I our partnership. But ye already knew, didn't ye?"

He grasped the professor by the lapels of his tweed suit jacket. "Ye had the foresight to know that with Till's view of the future of fairies, and by how quickly she learned everythin' anyone tried to teach her, that she was especially gifted."

"You, also, are especially gifted," Herrmann said at last, looking Gus straight in the eyes. "You know this."

Gus shrugged. "Try not to think of it. I just do my job."

"Until now," Herrmann retorted. "Now you don't want to just do your job. You want special dispensation to do whatever you want because the bill has come due for your reckless behavior and someone you love is paying. You had to know the risks, making Till your One Wish and making that wish something..." Color rose to his face and he waved his hand. He did not need to break the rules and delve into the private recesses of Gus's mind to elaborate on what he understood Gus had wished for. "Why don't you tell me exactly what it is that you want, Angus Duncan?"

Gus was sure the professor already knew the answer; he just wanted the request to be spoken. Gus answered without hesitation.

"I want ye to perform a bondin' ceremony for us. Right away."

Herrmann sighed so deeply and slowly Gus thought it would never end.

"I'll say it again," Gus took him by the shoulders and looked the man square in the face. "I am askin' ye to marry Till and I tonight, because I believe it's the only thing that will save her life."

"Then what happens?" Herrmann's eyes flashed fury, and he turned away. "The powers that be will take your gifts away, or at least severely diminish them…"

"If they can," Gus replied quickly. "I don't believe they are capable of it. Not this time. I am not my father, and Till…" He shook his head. "There is somethin' altogether different about Till. I don't know who in her family was hidin' the lineage, but there *has* to be more than just half fairy, half human to her. She is *gifted*, and she is killin' herself right now, moment by moment, trying to keep from me the fact that she remembers all that's been between us. I'm certain it's short circuiting her body."

"That's exactly what is happening," the professor said sadly. "Her body will burn itself out because it cannot handle the sheer amount of stress hormones being released into the system by the battle she has waged since…" Herrmann looked at Gus and let the unspoken question linger between them.

"New Year's Eve," Gus replied.

"Good heavens, she must be *incredibly* strong." Professor Herrmann began to pace. "She managed to keep from you that she remembered granting your One Wish all this time? How is that possible? How could you *not* know?"

"Denial casts a very powerful spell," Gus whispered, his voice heavy with regret. "All the signs were there. I knew she was keepin' somethin' serious from me. But never in my life before she just came out and said it in a moment of weakness did I *know*." His eyes filled with tears and he fought them back. She's been so strong, for such a long time..." He raised his gaze to the man, pleading. "Ye've got to help us, Professor Herrmann. Losin' her would be the death of me."

"It may be out of our hands, Gus," the professor replied softly. "It may already be too late."

"It's goin' to be too late for all of us soon if we don't at least try to take the next step!" Gus raised his voice now. "Ye know it to be true. Ye knew it well before Tilda Mae ever questioned ye in class that first day, that's why ye came down on her so hard. Ye *know*. And ye also know she is meant to be the start of the future for us all, not to perish by the antiquated rules of the past."

Herrmann was silent a long moment before finally continuing. "I know that they've been watching. Waiting," he replied at last. "Waiting for the right pair to come along. To risk allowing a complete bonding, to let the pair live as a couple and see how greatly it increased their abilities. But power is a dangerous thing, and those who have control fear losing it. What if they judge you as severely as your parents?"

"A risk I have no choice but to take," Gus insisted. "We may not be able to convince them 'til they see it for themselves. Until they see that a couple can have greater powers without abusin' them. To see what the strength of true love can do to increase fairy power, ten times. A hundred times. Who knows the limit?"

"That's what frightens me. No one knows." Professor Herrmann walked over to the door and held it open. "I'm sorry, I cannot help you."

"Then ye've damned us both," Gus said, moving swiftly past. "If she dies, I will surely follow."

Chapter Twenty-Six

Missing

THE MOMENT GUS REAPPEARED in Hannah's room, he knew something horrible had happened.

"No... please..." he whispered. The women were gone, and he began to look around the room for any clues as to where they'd disappeared to. Hannah must have failed to contact him, though given the way the room looked, with her furniture askew and everything that had been on the desk now on the floor, he knew she'd tried to resist whomever it was that had taken them.

Till must be unconscious again...

He shuffled through the debris and a faint glimmer caught his eye. He snatched up the bracelet in his hand and immediately recognized the charm attached to it.

"Lane," he whispered as he grasped the charm tightly in his hand, "I swear, if ye've hurt her, I am going to break *all the rules*."

"No you're not," a voice said from just behind him, and Gus turned to see Professor Herrmann standing there. The man bent down and picked something up from the floor: Till's shattered glasses. He wrapped his hands around them and instantly, they were mended. He held them out toward Gus. "Because we're going to find them."

Gus took the glasses and gently tucked them into the breast pocket of his jacket. He held Lane's bracelet out toward the professor. "This is going to help us do it."

Herrmann recognized the charm immediately. "Lane. I knew if anyone was going to interfere that it was going to be him."

"Do ye have any idea where they've gone?" Gus asked, handing the item over to Hermann for closer inspection.

"There have been stories for years, but even I have been unable to locate the board's mythical research facilities. That is where I think it's most likely Lane took her." Herrmann looked at him sadly. "And if you think I haven't been trying, for decades, to find them, then you underestimate my commitment to what's right."

"Research facilities?" Gus's anger grew. "There could be no good purpose for such a place."

Herrmann paled. "No, there couldn't. Why do you think I took such an interest in Till? I was worried about her from the day she arrived here, afraid she would draw the attention of the wrong people." He sighed as he looked at the charm on the bracelet. "I just had no idea at the time that Lane was one of those people."

"I was such a fool," Gus groaned. "I trusted him, even after past experience warned otherwise, because Aunt Tilda always trusted him."

"We all did."

Both men turned in shock at the sound of another voice behind them; one unfamiliar to Herrmann, but all too familiar to Gus.

"Liz, what the hell are you doin' here?"

"I regret my part in this, in *any* of this," Liz explained, her eyes bloodshot with unshed tears. "I know where he's taken her. I can take you there, but that is as far as I dare go."

"If that's all you're willin' to do, then I'll take it," Gus replied. "Where are they?"

"There is a secured space in what used to be the Science building. It's supposed to be storage." Her voice broke. "It is not."

Professor Herrmann whispered, "I can't believe it…"

"You didn't want to believe it, any of you." Bitterness replaced the fear in Liz's voice now. "The faculty, of all people, should have known. Should have stopped these things from happening. But you were all complicit, in my view, and that's why people like Lane have been able to do what they've done."

"Are ye goin' to take me to Till or not!" Gus shouted, and finally Liz took hold of one of his hands and one of Professor Herrmann's.

"Like I said," Liz replied through gritted teeth, "I can take you there, but I can't get you in. After that, you're on your own."

* * *

Gus shivered as they materialized just outside the old, retired Science building. It was a small, uninteresting thing; one would never suspect that it held anything more than unused office furniture.

"Stop Lane," Liz implored, "or it will mean the end for us all."

"What do you mean?" Herrmann pressed.

"He's sealed off the portal between DCTU and the human world," Liz replied, her voice devoid of emotion. "There's no way back now, not unless someone can stop him. We're trapped here... forever."

Professor Herrmann and Gus exchanged a disbelieving glance.

"Fine, don't believe me then! Try it, I dare you! Try to transport back. See what happens."

Professor Herrmann nodded to Gus, and closed his eyes. Sure enough, he went nowhere. "By the powers..." he whispered, looking at Gus with an entirely different expression now. The stakes had just become so much higher than the lives of two Fairy Godparents: the fate of their society rested on the shoulders of one man, and that man was Angus Duncan.

"Good luck," Liz said, and then she walked away.

"Who *was* that?" Herrmann asked.

"Later," Gus promised. "We have to figure out how to get inside."

The front door of the building appeared to be boarded up, and neither man could get through. Herrmann began scouting the darkened windows and brick exterior alike for a way in. He tried using his powers to open the latches on the windows, but none would move. "He must have a field up around the entire building," Herrmann said. "Can you get any kind of read on Till at all?"

"I can't. She must be unconscious, still."

"We have got to wake her up. Her powers combined with ours might be enough to open a window in, just a crack in the shielding, and help us find her. Without her help, I don't know what else we can do. We can't risk bringing anyone else into this," Herrmann said, answering Gus's next question before he was able to speak it. "We have to get you and Till bonded and safe before anyone else can find out what we're doing. It's a good thing that we've both put so much practice into shielding our thoughts over the years, Gus. Those powers are serving us well right now, and we dare not let them drop for an instant."

"Understood."

"Try to send a message, and I will too. To wake Till up."

Both men concentrated on those same three words:

Till, wake up.

A moment later Gus felt a pang of distress, a stabbing pain deep between his ribs, and inhaled sharply. He felt the sensation of Till's fear, deep and cold and dark, and immediately thought a message to her, hoping she'd hear him.

I'm coming, Till. Just hang on.

Slowly a thought crossed his mind. It was weak and weary, but it was definitely the voice he was seeking. *Gus, I'm afraid. I'm so tired.*

Ye've got to stay awake for me, Tilda Mae. Fight. Please, fight. And concentrate on one thought, three words only.

What?

Open the window, Till. We have got to open the window.

Gus became aware of the sound of another voice in his head now, chattering on at Till as she tried to focus.

"I don't know why I keep getting myself into trouble with human men," Hannah said, talking more to herself than anyone else. "No, wait, that's not true. I suppose in the end, I do know. The reason has always been the same, I guess." Hannah sighed, and Till tried to tune her out but had little success. "I keep getting into trouble because I would give anything, absolutely anything, to know what it's like to be loved, just once, the way that Gus loves you. You're so lucky, Till, and I am totally jealous."

Hannah! Gus thought sharply, making an attempt to quiet her. He figured then that it couldn't hurt to try to enlist her help as well; weak as her powers were, they might be enough to push them over the top.

What? Gus, is that you?

Open the window, Hannah. Tell Till. She has to think of openin' the window.

Till, no, no. Stay awake now… Hannah thought again, before her trail disappeared from Gus's consciousness.

"Just keep thinking that one thought, over and over, Gus," Professor Herrmann said, wiping perspiration from his brow with the cuff of his sleeve. "Open a window."

Gus tried to tune out the fact that as panicked as Till was, she was still fighting with all her might just to stay conscious.

I love ye, Till. Fight. Open a window. Then finally, one last thought. *Help me, Till…*

There was an unholy shattering sound as the window behind Gus and the professor exploded, glass flying free from the frame with astonishing force. Around it was a glowing white light with darkness at the center; she'd managed to punch a hole through the shielding around the building as well.

Both men covered their faces to keep the falling splinters out of their eyes.

"Well," Professor Herrmann said with a shake of his head when he could finally speak, "when she opens a window, she *really* opens a window."

"That noise would surely have alarmed someone," Gus worried. "Let's go."

"And then there are the alarms…"

"What!"

"We need to hurry."

"We need to shut 'em down, is what we need to do!" Gus retorted as they ran for the nearest staircase. "Wait, don't we WANT help to come? Security?"

"Not the 'security' these alarms send for. They're the board's equivalent of the goon squad." Herrmann replied, huffing a little as he rushed. "I'll try, but I can't make any promises."

Seconds later, the alarm stopped. "I've sent a 'false alarm' signal back to the monitoring station," he said, "but I am not certain if they'll buy it. I am also doing all I can to project a false all clear reading on the motion detectors…"

Gus nearly reeled as Till's thoughts invaded his mind again. She was trying very hard to focus them now, to muster as much strength as she was able to help guide him to her, and he heard faint echoes of a familiar, now sinister, voice in his head.

Are you afraid of me, Tilda Mae? You should be. There was a pause. *What about you, Hannah? Do you fear me? You should be very afraid of what I can, and will, do to be sure you never see the light of day again. No one here will ever see the sun again.*

I'm coming, Till. Help me find you, please, Gus thought, taking care not to project any of his raging thoughts in Lane's direction.

Fear… the word kept going through Till's mind as her thoughts faded in and out of Gus's perception.

Tilda Mae...

Fear, Gus. Fear... is... the key.

Gus changed directions sharply. He skidded around a corner and back the way they'd come, down the stairs until they took them as far as they would go: to the basement.

"What the hell are you hearing in that head of yours?" Professor Herrmann cried, and as he lost focus for a moment the alarm sirens wailed again.

"Just ye keep the alarms turned off and stay close!" Gus called, gaining speed as he ran.

He came to an abrupt stop and then backed up two doors. "This is it. They're in there."

"Are you sure?"

"Bet my life upon it."

"Help me... completely disable the alarms." The professor entreated, leaning back against the wall and struggling to catch his breath. "I can't keep them off much longer."

"I can't do it alone, not now..." Gus felt dizzy and tried again to grab onto Till's thoughts from the other side of the barrier. *Till, help me. The alarms...*

An instant later the pair heard a sizzling, popping noise, and they watched as a small box on the wall opposite them began to emit smoke. The alarms were stopped, for good.

"She has learned a thing or ten..."

"We're stronger together than we could ever be apart," Gus replied. "Now, to get in... I may not be able to take ye with me this time."

"You're not going to..."

"Hell yes I am! I am going to transport through the energy field Lane has put up around the room."

"You could be killed! Magic that powerful..."

"I'm already dead without Till," Gus declared. "Ye know that. So stand back, sir, and be ready to do what ye can, when the time comes."

Herrmann nodded and stood clear. "Good luck, Duncan."

Till, Gus thought, *I need to get in. Help me, darlin', I'm right outside...*

Gus concentrated, whispered a few words softly that the professor could not make out, and held his breath. He backed up as far as he could, and then, with Till's thoughts held as tightly as he could even as he sensed them slipping away, he took off running toward the metal security door. Just as he reached it, he vanished from sight.

With his powers and Till's combined, he managed to go straight through the door and the field Lane was struggling now to maintain, as he sensed he was losing control of the situation.

"Your Celtic prince has come to rescue, you Tilda Mae. How sweet, just like a real fairy tale. Only I'm afraid that this one isn't going to have a happy ending, for any of us."

"Definitely not for you, traitor," Gus gasped, struggling for breath. He dropped to his knees beside Till on the ground. "Till, can ye hear me, darlin'? I'm right here."

"She *can'na hear ye* now, Duncan," Lane taunted, circling the pair. "You're too late!"

"She went out again the moment you came through the door, Gus. I think she used every ounce of strength she had left to help get you here," Hannah said, surprising Gus with the fact that she had tears in her eyes. "Lane, I don't know what this is really about, but Gus and Till don't deserve to be here. If anyone does it's me, I'm the one who's on restriction—"

"You have no idea what you're talking about, Hannah, so just sit there quietly and you might get out of this yet with your life." He glared down at Gus, who now cradled Till in his arms and kissed the top of her head tenderly. "Till is definitely not going to be that lucky, and knowing his insufferably romantic ways, the Leprechaun will probably choose to die with her rather than try to live without her."

"Why are ye doin' this, Lane?" Gus asked, stroking Till's hair and then starting again to whisper in her ear, begging her to wake up. Surreptitiously, he used his powers to make the anklet he'd fastened on her vanish.

"Because you've broken the rules! Both of you! And if you're bonded as I think you are, then they're going to take your powers away anyway. Why suffer a long and drawn out end the way that your parents did? Why not just allow this dark chapter in fairy history to fade to black tonight? First with Till's death, then with yours."

Gus doubted, knowing the strength of their bond, that anyone could truly take his and Till's powers away now. If he could just get her through this and away from Lane's dark influence... everything would be all right.

"And if I chose to try to live without her?" Gus bluffed, knowing in his heart that he could do no such thing. He was simply trying every possible argument for the sake of keeping Lane talking while he held Till ever closer. If his theories were right, just being this near to him, with him constantly transferring thoughts of how much he loved her into her mind, Till should rally enough for them to attempt an escape, somehow.

"You would never, and even if you could, I'm afraid it's too late. I couldn't allow it."

"The rules!" Hannah shouted suddenly, leaping to her feet and rushing at Lane. She grasped hold of him by the shirt but was too weakened herself to do anything more than object. "You dare to talk about the code? The code says that another fairy is never to inflict violence except in self-defense. Gus isn't threatening you, you have no right to—"

"I have EVERY right!" Lane screamed. "His very existence is a threat to ALL of us! He was never supposed to exist! His parents broke the rules, but before they were brought to justice and the end they deserved, they created this unholy offspring… fairy, human, muse… I brought them to their ruin, and so I will do to you, as well."

"What?" Gus slowly set Till down and rose to his feet. "What did ye say?"

"The last secret is revealed!" Lane crowed. "*I* was the one who turned your parents in to the board! *I* was the one who pursued their case and saw to it that they were prosecuted."

Gus bolted forward. The sound that emanated from him was more than a scream; it was a battle cry. "BASTARD!" He grappled with Lane as Hannah moved toward Till, trying to shake her from her unconscious state.

"Till, wake up. Please, wake up!"

"You still don't get it, do you?" Lane growled, as he pushed Gus backward with shocking might and then raised both his arms, using his powers to slam Gus into the wall. Gus's head spun as he fought off the effects of the blow and valiantly countered Lane's assault. He summoned all his strength and managed to free himself from the grasp of Lane's dark magic, and the moment his boots hit the ground he rushed toward him again.

"If Till dies, so do you!" Gus shouted, frustrated as each attempted blow was now met and deflected by Lane.

"Insolent child! You can't begin to understand what is really going on here," Lane cried, stopping to turn toward Hannah. With one stroke in the air of a single finger, he brought the girl to her knees, overcome by the pain Lane was inflicting upon her. "This is not your war, Hannah. Stay where you are."

Lane released her from his grasp, but she was still too weakened by crippling pain to move: she could barely even breathe.

"Gus... and Till... have done nothing to you!" she choked between breaths. "There is no 'war'!"

"Nothing more is needed from you, little girl," Lane replied, and with another wave of his hand, Hannah's voice was silenced. She tried to speak, tried to scream, but no matter what she did, no sound issued from her lips. She raised her hand to her throat, eyes filling with tears as she attempted once again to fight her iron bonds, but still could not escape them.

"You have committed a crime against all of us! The greatest possible violation!" Lane spat, shaking Gus fiercely. "You have taken something that doesn't belong to you and expected to get away with it!"

"I don't know what the hell you're talking about!" Gus fought again to direct his powers toward Lane to free himself, but it was no use. His strength was fading with each passing second, and all he could think of was Till, lying so still in the corner, so close to leaving him forever.

In that split second of distraction, Lane took his chance to slam into Gus with a wicked blow. Gus was knocked back but kept to his feet. However, instead of escalating the fight now, he dropped, grasped hold of Till, and picked her up. "Hannah, get behind me," he instructed, and Hannah, for once in her life, did as she was told. She struggled to her feet and held onto Gus's shoulder.

"You cannot protect them, you cannot even protect yourself from my power," Lane raged, raising his hands and motioning toward Gus's throat. Gus closed his eyes and focused, and managed to counter Lane's attack, keeping his airway from collapsing.

For the moment, though, he chose to let Lane think that he was winning.

Hannah, watch carefully... be ready. Gus thought to her. Then he turned his mind to Till's again. *Till, darlin', hear me... if I have ever needed ye, I need ye now.*

He pressed his lips to her forehead and then whispered one last word in her ear in an attempt to reach her. "Please..."

Gus acted as though he was struggling for air, leaning back against the wall with Till still in his arms, before allowing her to gently slip from them and onto the floor.

"You're finished, Angus Duncan! The man who never should have been, the one they DARE to tell me is meant to do what I should have been able to do a century ago! I was the one who should have been the future of fairy kind. MY Tilda, and I... the FIRST Tilda, a hundred and fifty years ago! All those years I kept from her what she meant to me, and she didn't remember... she forgot... now she's gone. She died without ever remembering... but this one?" He pointed to Till. "This one fulfills your One Wish and never forgets! You both think you are so smart. There is no way that you could hide the fact that you were in love with each other from someone who knows what it REALLY means to suffer for love! Your future was supposed to be MINE!"

Ye can't control us anymore, Gus thought.

"Just watch me!" Lane screamed. "I don't need to for very much longer— soon your precious Tilda Mae will be dead, and so will you!"

Get ready, Hannah... Gus thought as he feigned the onset of unconsciousness. Then he sent out one more thought to the woman he'd risked everything for. *Tilda Mae, now!*

In that instant Till bolted upright, eyes wide open and afire with righteous indignation. She raised both her hands toward her nemesis and spoke the simple truth.

"I'm not afraid of you now!"

Lane flew across the room, smashing against the opposite wall with a sickening thump. His head snapped back against the brick and it was enough to knock him senseless.

"Hannah!" Gus shouted, hoping that her powers would be bolstered enough by his help and Till's to enable them to do what they needed to do.

"No!" Lane cried, realizing what was happening just as thick iron shackles appeared upon his wrists and ankles. Chains bound his limbs together, and the poisonous effect of the pure metal, while not enough to kill him, completely robbed him of his ability to use his powers.

The hum of electricity buzzed nearby as one by one the lights overhead flickered on and off before returning to their normal level of illumination; and it was then that they heard the door unlocking with a loud metallic clang.

"Love is stronger than hate, Lane, every time. And I promise y'er goin' to pay for what ye've done," Gus said, as the sound of Lane struggling against his bonds filled the room. "The very way ye've judged others, let ye now be judged."

Professor Herrmann rushed in, watching as Gus dropped back to the ground, completely spent, and lay beside Till. She was unconscious again, and this time so pale that Gus feared there would be no waking her.

If she had given her life for his... how could he possibly live with that?

Chapter Twenty-Seven
Bonded

PROFESSOR HERRMANN LOOKED AT GUS with urgency. "We'd best secure Lane here for now. I'll see to it that he faces the board of governors as soon as possible."

Lane withered down to a shadow of his former self, trapped in the prison he'd intended for others.

Gus was too busy to observe any feeling of victory. He took Till into his arms and pressed his lips to hers.

She remained still as stone.

"No...no..." Gus whispered. "Ye cannot leave me now, Tilda Mae. We've so much left to do." He brought her closer to his heart and kissed her again. Slowly, deeply, and with oceans and skies worth of love and passion he'd been fighting to hold back.

"Don't ye *dare* make a liar out of me," Gus pleaded, shaking Till gently before kissing her with greater desperation. "I told Lane that love wins every time. I can't live without ye, Tilda Mae. Please..." Tears filled his eyes as he began to lose hope. He closed them again and rested his forehead against hers. "I love ye. With all that I am. I always will."

He kissed her once more; fiercely, deeply, and with every last ounce of hope in his heart.

Finally, Till began to shake.

She tried to raise a hand up to touch him, but she was too weak. Seeing her react only spurred Gus on, and he continued kissing her until finally she gasped in a deep, resonant breath between them.

He smiled down at her through fresh tears, not caring who in the world saw his true love for her. "Time to wake up, darlin'. Ye have a weddin' to attend."

"Wedding?" Till asked, finally opening her eyes. "Whose wedding?"

"Ours." Gus's tears fell onto her face, and Till finally found the strength to touch him.

"But..."

"No more secrets, Tilda Mae," he whispered. "I *know*, and it's all right. It's all goin' to be all right now. I promise."

"Gus!" Her own tears rained down as she realized what he really meant. It was all over. She didn't have to pretend any more, she didn't have to fight against her very soul for his survival. Everyone would know the truth, and life, for them, would go on.

"We must go," Professor Herrmann interrupted. Without Lane's powers to hold them here, the professor easily teleported them back to his home.

Gus still held Till in his arms, and Hannah stood by, observing, wiping at her eyes with the back of her hand.

"Now, I believe you wished me to perform a bonding ceremony," Professor Herrmann said, actually doing something Gus had never seen in all the time he'd known the man. He was smiling.

"Please, and thank ye, sir. If ye'd be so kind."

"No time to lose. The sooner the bonding is complete, the stronger she'll become."

"My parents..." Till whispered, her head lolling slightly against Gus's shoulder. He kissed her again, the strength he imparted to her by doing so allowed her to focus.

"We'll have a weddin' back there, I promise, Till. But this, my darlin', can't wait."

Gus dropped down to his knees on the floor, still holding Till in his arms.

"Hannah, you'll be witness to the event?" Professor Herrmann asked.

"It would be my honor," she said, grateful to have her voice back, and speaking sincerely for once in her life.

Professor Herrmann moved to stand before them, and gestured for Hannah to take her place beside Till.

"In ancient days, bondings were moments of the greatest possible joy in the Fairy world," he began. "Then darkness fell upon us all, and our greatest joy became our deepest heartache." He bowed his head soberly and was silent a moment before continuing. "Those who abused privilege cost us all something dear, and centuries have been spent trying to right their wrongs by living in denial of the truth: that a pair of Fairy Godparents, truly joined and bonded souls, cannot be separated by law. Their love remains, and as we have now seen, cannot be denied even in the face of certain death.

"So this night, an antiquated law will be broken, along with the powerful, dark magic that it has created. One couple has been chosen by the powers to take the first step into a brave era of renewal, and I am humbled and honored to acknowledge their bond and declare it official now, and for all eternity.

"Angus Cailan Duncan, is it your wish to be bonded to Tilda Mae Nesbitt for the remainder of your days? To love and protect her; be her comforter, companion, rescuer and confidant in this life, and in the life awaiting?"

"It is my wish," Gus declared. He brought Till's hand to his lips and kissed it softly.

"So may it be." The professor nodded.

Gus closed his eyes and concentrated for a moment, and a beautiful set of wedding rings appeared upon Till's left hand: a classic, antique-style diamond engagement ring and a wide white gold band with Celtic symbols engraved upon it.

Till gasped, her eyes shining as she gazed at them, then back at Gus. He was so happy in this moment, he felt his heart might not be able to contain it all. He could feel her strength growing by the second. Professor Herrmann's voice broke the silence.

"Tilda Mae Nesbitt, is it your wish to be bonded to Angus Cailan Duncan for the remainder of your days? To love and protect him; be his comforter, companion, rescuer and confidant in this life, and in the life awaiting?"

"It is... my wish." Till whispered. She grasped Gus as tightly as she could, adding, "It always was my wish. I know that now." She closed her eyes and an identical wedding band to hers appeared upon Gus's left hand.

Gus kissed her forehead, unable, in this moment, to speak.

"We'll forego the part about anyone having any objections to this union, as I think we all know the answer to that question..." Herrmann muttered, before clearing his throat and speaking with conviction once again. "In that case, it is my solemn duty and honor to decree that Angus Cailan Duncan and Tilda Mae Nesbitt have been joined and irrevocably bonded to one another, in this life, and the life awaiting. May the powers bless you both, and protect you on your path."

"May it be so," Hannah added, bowing her head.

Gus and Till stared into each other's eyes, and Gus felt Till's strength growing by the moment. Barrier after barrier in her mind fell before him, crashing down and freeing up her powers and mental abilities to return her to health. Her body no longer suffered the continual punishment of trying to hide the truth from him; and in that instant, her healing truly began.

Gus was overcome by the strength of her love for him, and the force of one specific memory...

They were standing in the shadows behind the Music building, and she had just confessed to him that her One Wish was for one perfect kiss from him; that was when he had told her that his One Wish was one perfect night with her. Till had been right, he had kissed her, and for the very first time, in starlight on the campus of Dreams Come True University...

Oh, Till, my darlin'...

"You can kiss her now, Gus," Hannah whispered, nudging him none too gently.

Gus didn't just embrace Till, he grasped her to his heart and kissed her with the singular kind of tenderness that supersedes all heartache.

"I love ye, Tilda Mae," he whispered, burying his face in her hair.

"I love you too," she whispered back. "Please, let's go home."

"Soon, darlin', soon." Gus nodded his thanks to the professor, who lowered his eyes.

"I only did what was right, Mister Duncan."

"Ye saved us both, and for that I shall be forever in yer debt." His eyes moved toward Hannah and then back to the professor. "What happens now?"

"I will speak to the board... explain all of this," Herrmann answered. "You live your lives, and we all stand back and watch. Be careful, whatever you do. Respect the powers bestowed upon you, and never let them change you."

Gus nodded. "And Hannah?"

"Yeah, what about Hannah?" Hannah asked.

"I think I will be intervening on her behalf as well," Herrmann said.

"Yay!" Hannah jumped up and down and placed a kiss upon Gus's cheek. Then she looked down at Till, whose head was resting against Gus's chest. "Did you rent out my room yet?"

"Not… yet… but I might," Till teased. Then she closed her eyes, and Gus knew he needed to get her home. Their bonding must be completed to assure her safety.

"My thanks, to ye both, for everythin'," Gus said, and then, he and Till were gone.

Soon he was placing her gently on her bed — their bed — and kissing her again.

He thought momentarily that he wished he'd filled the room with roses; and as the merest idea crossed his mind, vase after vase of perfect, fragrant long-stemmed roses in every color imaginable began to appear on each available surface in the room. Stands of candles burned alongside them, and when Gus looked down at Till again, she was no longer wearing the simple dress she had been, but instead a pure white peignoir made of silk and trimmed with lace.

"Whoa," Gus said, shaking his head to clear the thought, but no matter how he tried, it remained; and so did everything he'd imagined into being. "Goin' to have to be careful now, seems my thoughts suddenly have a hair trigger."

Till did something so disarming, something that made her so desirable, he thought his heart would break all over again. She laughed. Not her usual laugh, but one that was deeper and much more sensual. It was maddening, it was incredible, and it left him defenseless.

"They're beautiful, thank you," she whispered. She caressed his face as he lowered himself down beside her. Immediately her arms encircled him. "I never could forget you, Gus. I never could forget *this*." She slid his jacket down over his shoulders and reached for the buttons on his shirt. Gus shivered.

"I belonged to ye from the moment I saw ye, Tilda Mae," he whispered as his breath grew short. "I always will."

He ran his hand through her hair and across the line of her jaw, tracing the stroke with a trail of gentle kisses, growing in intensity as he moved. He felt more alive in this moment than he ever had before.

Her strength returned to a greater degree with every touch, and he could sense their gifts combining into something that neither could quite fathom yet. Joined and bonded, their hearts, souls, and powers would increase in ability and work in concert. No wonder the thought struck fear into the souls of those without such a source of inner strength.

"I need you, Gus," Till whispered, as he exhaled softly in her ear.

"Ye'll never be without me again, Till," he vowed, as he tenderly drew the strap of her nightgown away from her skin. "Promise ye that."

* * *

Till rested against Gus's chest once again, his arms wrapped tightly around her. Gus sensed happiness in her she'd never known and understood, because not only did he feel it in every single thought and emotion she radiated, but he felt the same way, too.

"So beautiful," she said, staring at her rings a moment before sighing. "How are we ever going to explain this to my parents?"

"I'm sure they'll understand that we were not the first couple swept away in the moment who ran away to get married," Gus replied, placing a kiss atop her head.

"You ran to do so much more than get married..." She kissed his cheek softly. "You saved my life."

"To lose yer life would have been to lose my own," he whispered. "Ye may believe y'er the one who was saved, but ye don't know what my life was like before ye were in it..." He slid his fingers through the silken strands of her hair as he spoke. "It was so empty; I was alone and always thought I would be. That I'd never be able to share my heart with anyone, not only because of the rules against it, but because there was no one who could ever reach me."

He thought back to how dark his outlook had been before he knew Till; how he just kept doing his job to the best of his ability, but not being able to understand, truly, the point. No matter what he said or what anyone else thought, he was a lonely man, adrift. Then she was there, and suddenly he had not just a reason to do the job, but a reason to *be*. Loving Till, teaching her and protecting her to the best of his ability, gave him a reason to exist.

"Ye gave me a reason to try, and I promise I will always try my best for ye. No matter what ye need, I will find a way to give it to ye."

"I just need you," Till whispered, as the thoughts of exactly what she needed raced across her mind and into his.

The thought that next crossed his mind brought tears to Till's eyes, which shined on him more brightly than any stars he'd ever seen.

I need you, too.

"I love ye, Tilda Mae," he gasped. "So much."

Till ran her hand gently up and down his arm and Gus trembled. No matter how or when she touched him, he always had the same reaction: she was irresistible.

"What happens now?" Till asked, watching the first light of morning stream in through the window to greet the day. "They won't try to take our powers away, like they did to your parents?"

"They can't do it to us, Till. We're different. What we have is unique, even Professor Herrmann knows it. Lane knew it, that's one of the reasons he was dead set against it." He gave her a slow, lingering kiss before continuing. "Our powers will keep growin' stronger, and we will be faced with the responsibility of managing them wisely and usin' them only when justified."

"I would have died to protect you, you know," Till said, as she ceased watching the light flicker upon her rings and stared into his eyes again. "I would have done anything to keep you safe."

"You did, Tilda Mae. You did protect me, and I will spend the rest of my life returnin' the favor."

Chapter Twenty-Eight
The Most Powerful Magic of All

TILL HELD GUS'S HAND IN A GRIP so tight she was cutting off the circulation to his fingers as they walked up to the back door of Happily Ever After Books.

"Mom is going to freak," she sighed.

"It's more y'er father that worries me, but I'll take care of it. Don't ye worry yer pretty head about it."

Till blushed. She couldn't remember Gus ever calling her pretty out loud before, even though she'd caught him thinking it at least a dozen times in the past hour alone. In fact, he'd even thought her beautiful. It was something she wasn't used to, and Gus knew that.

Ye'll get used to it, darlin'. I'll keep tellin' ye until ye do, and even then I'll keep tellin' ye, he thought.

"I love you, Gus," she said.

"I love ye too."

Till used her key to open the door in case her mother was standing on the other side and magic would be discovered.

Sure enough, Mrs. Nesbitt stood there, tapping her toe.

"I suppose it is too much trouble for either of you to call me and tell me you're still alive, if you're going to stand me up two days in a row," she shrieked. "I was about to file a police report, you know! Where on earth have you... two... been?" Her words slowed to a stop as Gus gently picked up Till's hand and held it out toward her mother, displaying her wedding rings.

Mrs. Nesbitt blinked once, twice, three times, and then she screamed. "Arthur! Arthur, get in here!"

Till's father came rushing out of the office as fast as he could move. "Clara? What is..." He looked at Till and Gus and sighed with relief. "Thank heavens you're all right. You really had us worried."

"Sorry, sir, we were in our own little world for a while, I'm afraid," Gus said softly. "We... did somethin' that I hope the two of ye can forgive us for. I should have asked in advance for yer blessin', and I regret that I didn't, but I'm askin' for it now, sir because, well, Tilda Mae and I... we..."

"We *eloped*!" Till cried, throwing her arms around her father and mother.

"You what...?" Her father began, but Mrs. Nesbitt was quick to intervene. She released Till and grasped Gus into a great, nearly suffocating hug.

"My wish came true! I don't believe it, but it came true!" she cried. "I'm so happy!" She wiped away joyful tears. "Now don't think that this gets you two out of having a proper wedding, but other than that, I couldn't be happier!"

"Sir?" Gus inquired softly of Till's father. His lips were clenched and his eyes were focused on Gus.

"Dad," Till begged, putting her arms around his neck. "You always said you just wanted me to be happy? I'm happy. Please, be happy for us."

The old man's eyes turned red and he nodded. "I guess I will have to start calling you 'son' now?"

"Ye can call me whatever ye like, sir," Gus laughed, taking Till into his arms once again and kissing her forehead. "Just as long as I get to keep her."

* * *

August 12, 2013

Gus tapped a booted foot as he waited impatiently at the end of the flower-lined aisle. The yard outside the house had never looked more lovely, and he and Till couldn't imagine anywhere in the human world where they would rather be married than on the spot where they'd first met; the day she found out what she was really meant to become, while Gus was sweeping away the newly fallen snow.

He shifted back and forth and tried to steady his nerves. Wasn't it ever going to be time?

In his head, he heard the sound of Till's voice as she thought something to him from inside the house, where she was putting the finishing touches on.

I love you...

"I love ye, darlin'," Gus whispered softly in reply, much to the amusement of the person who had just stepped up beside him.

"Thank you, Duncan, but really, is that appropriate?" The man teased, actually making a joke for the first time Gus could ever remember. "You look pale, son. You're not having second thoughts?"

A grin spread across Gus's face. Professor Herrmann had not only made a very rare trip into the human world to attend today, but he had even shown up in a kilt and matching jacket and shirt to Gus's so he'd look the part that Gus wished him to play: that of best man.

"Not for an instant," Gus replied. "It's awfully good to see ye, sir," Gus extended his hand. "Apologies, it's a bit sweaty."

"Any man who can get married without sweaty palms is not taking the oath seriously enough," Professor Herrmann replied with a slight smile. He sent a thought to Gus, and Gus thought back to him loud and clear.

Never regretted it for a moment. I know it's right.

"I believe it's right, too," the professor replied. "That's why I'm here. Besides, someone has to keep an eye on you two."

"No one else I would rather trust with that duty, sir," Gus said sincerely.

"We're about ready to begin," the officiant announced, approaching Gus and extending his hand toward the professor. "Ah, I see the best man has arrived. And you are?"

"William Herrmann, friend of the family. Pleased to meet you," Professor Herrmann said, shaking the officiant's hand. "And I think you're right. Gus, look." He gestured toward the house and Gus saw Hannah emerge first. She smiled at Gus and gave him a wink.

Déjà vu all over again, eh Leprechaun? At least this time I'm properly dressed, she thought to him, and Gus laughed softly.

Thank ye, Hannah...

His thoughts — and his heart — stopped for a second when he looked up again and saw Till on her father's arm.

She looked every bit the angel he knew her to be, dressed in a gown of pure white lace. Tears formed in the corner of his eyes, and he blinked them away with the memory of how afraid he'd been that he'd lose her— of how losing her would have meant losing everything.

She beamed as she walked toward him, and when she reached the end of the aisle he grasped hold of her hands and wouldn't let go.

Are you ready to make wishes come true? she thought to him, tears shining in her own eyes as well.

"As long as ye love me," he whispered, leaning close, "I am ready for whatever may come."

* * *

Gus glanced over at his beloved Tilda Mae. She was so peaceful now, glowing with joy and radiating an energy that he'd never felt from her before.

She was truly content, in this moment, here with him. Her heart was no longer divided against itself, battling her love for him. She was finally whole.

She was the most beautiful thing he'd ever seen, and her emotions were more captivating than any experience he'd ever known.

He took her away from everyone as the last of the stragglers left, and drew her farther back into the yard. She followed wordlessly where he led, satisfied to go wherever he would take her.

"Too bad about the clouds," she whispered at last, as she read his thoughts and knew what was in them. "We get married the night of the Perseids, so it will always be near our anniversary, and yet on our wedding night the view gets called on account of weather."

"Or so ye think," Gus whispered, stopping and standing in the clearing between trees at the very back of the yard. The nighttime air was fragrant and laced with a trace of humidity, and his cheeks took on color as his heart beat ever faster at her nearness.

He drew her slowly into his arms and then glanced up toward the heavens. "Look."

Till gasped and held her breath in wonder as the cloud cover began to part, just enough to allow them a clear patch of sky to see the meteors race past.

Colorful streaks illuminated the heavens, and Gus leaned in and captured Till's tears with kisses as they trailed down her cheeks, one by one.

"How are you doing that?" Till asked breathlessly, though she knew the answer. Even she was amazed by how strong his abilities had become; he was actually changing the atmosphere, just for her. She shook her head. "Magic."

"Till, yer love is the most powerful magic I have ever known."

"Hold me tighter," Till said, turning away from the shimmering lights long enough to bury her face in his shoulder.

"Don't worry, my darlin'. I'm right here, and I'm never going to let go." He grasped her closer still, lifting her in his arms until her feet barely touched the ground. "Ye *are* magic," he declared. "Now all *my* wishes have come true."

THE END

Acknowledgments

This book would not exist if not for the talent, generosity, and kindness of a team of people unlike any other I have ever known. Without their specialized help, time, care, and attention, it simply would not be.

Therefore I would like to express my heartfelt thanks to everyone at Booktrope, but especially to my team: Katherine Sears, Wendy Logsdon, Jennifer Gracen, Steven Luna, Adam Bodendieck, Ida Jansson, Jesse James Freeman, and Victoria Wolffe.

Without all of you, Gus and Till would not have their ending; and I am grateful to you beyond measure.

F.G.

ALSO BY FEBRUARY GRACE

Of Stardust (Fantasy) At the age of twenty-six single, geeky bookseller Till Nesbitt inherits the shock of a lifetime: a huge Victorian farmhouse filled with unique tenants, and the knowledge that there is a reason she's always been different. She's destined to become a fairy godmother, because the skills are written into her DNA.

Godspeed (Steampunk) In a steam-powered society, medical advancement is the last forbidden frontier. Can a young doctor working in secret rebuild his shattered heart by saving that of another? Or will ghosts of the past rise again, endangering all he holds dear?

MORE GREAT READS
FROM BOOKTROPE

The Chosen (Book One of the Portals of Destiny Series) **by Shay West** (Fantasy) To each of the four planets are sent four Guardians, with one mission: to protect and serve the Chosen, those who alone can save the galaxy from the terrifying Meekon. An epic story of life throughout the galaxy, and the common purpose that brings them together.

Dead of Knight **by Nicole J. Persun** (Fantasy) King Orson and King Odell are power-stricken, grieving, and mad. As they wage war against a rebel army led by Elise des Eresther, it appears as though they're merely in it for the glory. But their struggles are deeper and darker.

Doublesight **by Terry Persun** (Fantasy) In a world where shape shifters are feared, and murder appears to be the way to eliminate them, finding and destroying the source of the fear is all the doublesight can do.

Discover more books and learn about our new approach to publishing at **booktrope.com**.

Made in the USA
Lexington, KY
30 May 2016